WINGS OF FIRE

A GUIDE TO THE DRAGON WORLD

BY **TUI T. SUTHERLAND**

ILLUSTRATED BY **JOY ANG**

MAPS AND ADDITIONAL ART BY **MIKE SCHLEY**
ADDITIONAL COLOR BY **MAARTA LAIHO**

SCHOLASTIC PRESS
NEW YORK

For Joy Ang, whose incredible artwork brought all
these dragons to life, and for Phil Falco, who has made
these books so beautiful from the very beginning;
I am in awe of both of you!

With special thanks to Sarah Evans, Mike Schley, Maarta Laiho, and Carol Ly

Text copyright © 2023 by Tui T. Sutherland

Illustrations by Joy Ang © 2023 Scholastic Inc.
Pages iv–v (background), 6, 9, 10, 21 (bottom), 31, 32, 35, 45, 51, 52, 55–58, 61, 64,
67, 69, 72, 75, 77, 84, 87, 88, 95, 106, 108, 111, 112, 113, 116, 119, 131, 132, 135, 136–137, 138,
141, 142, 148, 149, 150, 153, 154, 157, 163, 164–165, 166, 173, 176, 178, 181, 186–187, 188,
193, 194, 197, 198, 201–203, 207, 210, 214, 217, 219, 221, 231, 232–233 (background)

Maps and additional art © 2012–2023 by Mike Schley
Pages i, iii, v, 4–5, 8, 17, 21, 34, 46–47, 48, 50, 53, 54, 60, 62, 86, 100, 105, 107, 110,
114–115, 117, 134, 156, 158, 159, 160, 161, 174–175, 180, 196, 204, 216, 230

Additional color by Maarta Laiho
Pages 4–5, 8, 9, 17, 21, 34, 35, 53, 54, 60, 61, 86, 87, 100, 105, 107, 110, 111, 134,
135, 156, 157, 159, 161, 174–175, 180, 181, 196, 197, 216, 217, 230, 231

"SkyWing Anthem" © 2023 by Adam Sterns

All rights reserved. Published by Scholastic Press, an imprint of Scholastic Inc., *Publishers since 1920*. SCHOLASTIC,
SCHOLASTIC PRESS, and associated logos are trademarks and/or registered trademarks of Scholastic Inc.

The publisher does not have any control over and does not assume any
responsibility for author or third-party websites or their content.

No part of this publication may be reproduced, stored in a retrieval system,
or transmitted in any form or by any means, electronic, mechanical, photocopying, recording,
or otherwise, without written permission of the publisher. For information regarding permission, write
to Scholastic Inc., Attention: Permissions Department, 557 Broadway, New York, NY 10012.

This book is a work of fiction. Names, characters, places, and incidents are either the
product of the author's imagination or are used fictitiously, and any resemblance to actual persons,
living or dead, business establishments, events, or locales is entirely coincidental.

Library of Congress Cataloging-in-Publication Data available

ISBN 978-1-338-63482-2

10 9 8 7 6 5 4 3 2 1   23 24 25 26 27

Printed in China   62
First printing, October 2023

Book design by Phil Falco

TABLE OF CONTENTS

CHAPTER ONE
MUDWINGS
7

CHAPTER TWO
SEAWINGS
33

CHAPTER THREE
RAINWINGS
59

CHAPTER FOUR
NIGHTWINGS
85

CHAPTER FIVE
SANDWINGS
109

CHAPTER SIX
ICEWINGS
133

CHAPTER SEVEN
SKYWINGS
155

CHAPTER EIGHT
SILKWINGS
179

CHAPTER NINE
HIVEWINGS
195

CHAPTER TEN
LEAFWINGS
215

FELLOW DRAGONS,

We have been researching the tribes and kingdoms of our world for some time now, and it has become clear to us that none of the previous scrolls that claimed to be "guides" to our world were remotely adequate or complete enough.

Many of the current scrolls in our libraries were written by NightWings or SeaWings (or in the case of Pantala, the HiveWings), giving us a necessarily limited view of all the other tribes. Many of these guides, for instance, do not include anything about RainWing venom or LeafWing leafspeak. They describe all SkyWings as unfriendly, all RainWings as lazy, all MudWings as thickheaded, and all SandWings as sly and underhanded. One would think this could go without saying, but just to be clear: *Every dragon is an individual*. You cannot lump all the dragons from any tribe into one category. That is closed-minded nonsense, and exactly the sort of thinking that the Jade Mountain Academy was founded to fight against.

Therefore, we have decided to embark upon the following project: to compile a more true, more complete, more representative guide to *all* the dragons of our world.

Starflight, our head librarian and archivist of the Jade Mountain Academy, is launching an outreach expedition to every tribe: from the palaces and strongholds to the border towns, outer islands, and smallest villages. We are asking for your voices and stories and the details of everyday dragon life: anything that should be included in a real Guide to the World of Dragons.

Thank you for your help with this book! We hope it brings joy and greater understanding to everyone who reads it!

Signed,

Tsunami, Sunny, Starflight, Clay, and Queen Glory

Starflight means the other scrolls were bad! And SO BORING, you guys! I've seriously used *The NightWing Guide to the Dragons of Pyrrhia* to put myself to sleep, like, 800 times.
— Fatespeaker

In case you can't tell, Sunny and Glory helped write this section.
— **Fatespeaker**

And then Starflight took out most of the yelling bits and made it sound all polite!
— Glory

And me, Fatespeaker! And Peril says also her, ~~although what she has to do with~~ because she is VERY helpful and good for morale and hasn't set anyone on fire in AGES, a thing that could change if you don't write down exactly what I'm saying hey what are you writing now stop that give me that

You should have seen the fight Sunny and Starflight had over this last exclamation point! It was very funny. Sunny totally won.
— **Fatespeaker**

We are MAKING THE WORLD A BETTER PLACE! Of COURSE there should be EXCLAMATION POINTS!!!
— Sunny

Although many learned dragons question our stories of the Scorching, it is still a key part of our history — the moment we measure time from, the foundation of our understanding of the world. While we may not know how much of the legend is true, it is still a fascinating tale to study and debate. — **Starflight**

THE LEGEND OF THE SCORCHING

Once upon a time, when the world was newly hatched, there were no dragon kingdoms. There were no dragon tribes. There were no dragon towns, no villages, no palaces or strongholds or cities.

Dragons of that day and age were solitary creatures. You might find one living alone in a mountain cave, or a small family on an icy island in the distant north, or a pair in a canyon deep under the sea.

But if you walked the land of Pyrrhia or flew through its skies, what you would find easily, everywhere you went, were scavengers. The forests teemed with scavengers, and their dens were everywhere. A dragon could barely set its talons down anywhere without landing on a scavenger. Scavengers strutted the world as though it was theirs.

And for the most part, dragons did not care. As long as they could be left alone, with enough prey to eat and some treasure to hoard, dragons were content to keep to their caves.

The scavengers, however, were not content. They scrabbled out of their dens and went scavenging for more than what they had. They killed the dragons' prey and choked the skies with smoke, and then, worst of all, they came for the dragons' treasure. Scavengers snuck into caves and sailed to the dragon islands and climbed the tallest trees of the jungle to find even the most hidden dragons. They stole gold, emeralds, sapphires, and pearls; they stole narwhal horns and rare fruit seeds and small sentimental wood carvings. If a dragon could count it as treasure, the scavengers would try to steal it.

Sometimes they came in groups. Sometimes they brought weapons. And sometimes they went too far.

No one knows why a scavenger would steal a dragon egg.

But we know he stole it from the wrong dragon.

Her original name is lost to time, but she was a dragon of immense strength and cunning: older, wiser, and more dangerous than most. Her lair was high in the mountain peaks, one of the very last to be found by the marauding scavengers.

And when they stole her egg, her wrath blazed as fierce as the lightning; her roar shook the mountains like thunder.

Alone, she could find the thieves and eat them. She could burn a scavenger den and have some measure of vengeance. But she wanted more.

And so she found the other dragons. She sought them out and brought them into her army. One by one, from across the world, they joined together under her wings. They became her talons and her claws and her ferocious teeth.

And they began to scorch the earth.

They burned the scavengers out of their holes; they set their dens ablaze. They took back their treasure and they took back the land.

They were the first dragon tribe.

And she became known as the first Dragon Queen.

When the Scorching was complete, the scavengers who survived scattered into hidey-holes across the world. Powerless, insignificant, no more than prey, as they should have been all along.

The world now belonged to dragons, and would for the rest of time.

Queen Snowfall's
Palace

Where-the-Whales-
Leap-at-Dawn

Where-the-Terns-Fly

Ice Kingdom

Among-the-Evergreens

Sky Kingdom

Where-No-Dragon-
Goes-Hungry

Possibility

Claws of the
Clouds Mountains

Queen Thorn's
Stronghold

Sanctuary

Kingdom of
Sand

Darkstalker's Teeth

Scorpion Den

Jade Mountain

Abandoned Ancient
Nightwing Palace

Talon Peninsula

Renewal

CHAPTER 1

MUDWINGS

QUEEN MOORHEN
AT THE MUDWING PALACE

MUDWINGS

SCALES: brown, sometimes with amber and gold underscales

EYES: brown, amber, or hazel

UNUSUAL CHARACTERISTICS: large flat heads with nostrils on top of the snout; thick armored scales

ABILITIES: can breathe fire (if warm enough); hold their breath for up to an hour;
blend into large mud puddles; usually very strong

HABITAT: the swamps, marshes, and boiling mud pools between the mountains and the sea

DIET: crocodiles, water birds, hippos, water buffalo, cows, elephants,
really anything they can get their claws on

QUEEN: Queen Moorhen

As a librarian, sometimes I am very attached to the scrolls I grew up with — some would say *too* attached. I stocked the Jade Mountain Academy library with all the scrolls that were familiar to me, including the following, and with scrolls that were handed to me by my own guardians. But in my first year as school librarian, a young MudWing named Sepia taught me a valuable lesson: to think more carefully about *who is telling a particular story*, *why*, *and whether their point of view can be trusted* — or whether there might be voices out there who could give us something more true.

That is why I decided to include the following scroll with its notes. While I can NEVER condone writing on a library scroll (the HORROR), in this case Sepia was trying to tell me something too important to ignore.

— Starflight

THE SLUGLIKE QUALITIES OF MUDWINGS

BY WISEMIND OF THE NIGHTWINGS

MudWings: the slowest and dimmest of all the tribes. Imagine slugs that blorped their way onto land and developed wings, and you'll have the right general idea.

The average adult MudWing dragon is large and quite strong. Their armored scales and ability to breathe fire (when they are the correct temperature) make them fairly useful in battle, as long as they can be roused from their mud puddles. If given the choice, the typical MudWing would prefer to stay submerged in mud, sleeping the day away, with only their snout poking out of their swamp. When they are awake, the MudWing generally passes the time lazing about with friends.

If pressed, the MudWing is capable of swimming underwater without pausing for breath for up to an hour at a time. Generally, however, MudWings expend their limited energy only to procure food, preferring slow-moving cows or crocodiles scooped up from their muddy swamps.

Careful observation of MudWings in their native swamp habitat has revealed little else of note about these sluglike dragons.

More like SMUGmind or EMPTYmind or ThinksHeKnows EverythingBut Actually DOESN'TMind.

Sleeping in mud makes us stronger! It's warm and lovely and it helps us heal if we get hurt, especially in battle. I bet this NightWing never fought a day in their life, and he sure doesn't know anything about what it's like to be a MudWing.

Any dragon who thinks crocodiles are slow-moving has CLEARLY never tried to catch one.

ARRRGH AS IF this NightWing knows ONE SINGLE ACTUAL THING about us! Has he ever SPOKEN to a MudWing? Spent any time in a MudWing village? Asked us our opinions about anything? I bet my bigwings could SQUASH HIM in a flying race AND on any intelligence test!

This is REALLY RUDE, even for those of us who actually like slugs!

If by lazing about with friends, you mean *training hard with my siblings*, why, yes, that IS how I spent most of my time. At least until I came to school, where I work EXTREMELY hard at everything I do and got the highest score in the Silver Winglet in Persuasive Essay Writing!

"Careful observation" means "spying from a distance and never actually talking to a single MudWing." This snooty NightWing knows NOTHING about my amazing tribe!!

Sepia,

Fatespeaker alerted me to the notes you wrote in the margins of our library scroll The Sluglike Qualities of MudWings. *I must admit I was rather horrified — a library scroll! Sepia! A LIBRARY SCROLL! But then I had Fatespeaker read me your notes, and I realized that you are actually saying something crucially important.*

For one thing, you are right: This is a distressingly biased, inaccurate NightWing report. The dragon who wrote it clearly had a "NightWings are superior" attitude and it is abundantly evident that they never spoke to any MudWings before writing the scroll.

I sent Fatespeaker on a quest to count all the scrolls written by MudWings in our library, and she found . . . two. Out of all these scrolls, only two by MudWings! Well. This is a problem a librarian can solve! Clearly we need to acquire more scrolls written by dragons about their own tribes and their own experiences. Firsthand accounts are an essential way for dragons to learn about one another.

With this in mind, I have an assignment for you. I would like you to write a scroll about MudWing siblings for us to add to the library. I think other tribes could learn a lot from your personal perspective, and I would be proud to include your voice in our library's collection.

(But no more writing on library scrolls! If you find any more scrolls you have concerns about, please come talk to me or Fatespeaker instead!)

— Starflight

Let's go with a more library-appropriate title, if that's all right, Sepia?
— Starflight

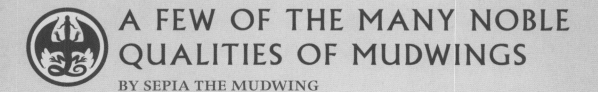

A FEW OF THE MANY NOBLE QUALITIES OF MUDWINGS

BY SEPIA THE MUDWING

During the War of SandWing Succession, lots of dragons noticed how strong, brave, and true MudWing troops are. Most dragons don't seem to know that this is because each troop is made up of brothers and sisters — all siblings from the same hatching. MudWing siblings are always together, starting from the day their eggs are snuggled into their warm and cozy mud nests.

In each sibling troop, the first-born dragon is the bigwings. They are the biggest and strongest and the natural leader of their troop. During hatching, the bigwings climbs out of their egg first and immediately goes to help their brothers and sisters break out of their own shells. A good bigwings takes care of their siblings and makes sure they learn a lot and grow up to be brave, kind dragons.

For the rest of their lives, the troop of siblings will live together, hunt together, and train together. When they have to fight, they follow their bigwings into battle. Usually each troop will also have:

- A healer (who studies the medicinal uses of mud and various leaves)

- A treasurer (who keeps track of the troop's shared treasure and provisions)

- A gatherer (who finds additional food to add to the prey they all hunt together)

- A communicator (who takes on the task of negotiating with other troops or asking for help if necessary)

Who gets which assignment depends on our natural skills and preferences. (I'm the communicator in my troop, *obviously*. My brother Newt is our healer, which is why he also chose to come to the academy, to learn about the medical discoveries of other tribes.) And sometimes the bigwings will be in charge of one of those areas, too, if they're really good at something like math, like my bigwings sister is.

Sometimes MudWings lose sibs, which is the worst thing that could ever happen to anyone. This happened a lot during the War, and it was really sad, and many troops are still recovering from those losses. An incomplete sib group might look for unsibs — dragons who have lost one or more of their own — to join their group.

Being part of a troop is one of the best things about being a MudWing. No other tribe bonds with their brothers and sisters like we do, which makes MudWings very special and pretty definitely the most loyal, caring tribe in all of Pyrrhia.

Dearest, cleverest Starflight,

I hope you make someone read you this letter at ONCE, even though I can't imagine anyone else at the academy reads with as much expression as I do! I have been worrying and worrying about you because all my visions are telling me that you miss me so dreadfully. I had one the other day where you were just lying on a window seat in the library, with your noble nose pointed at the sky, sighing and murmuring, "Fatespeaker . . . oh, Fatespeaker . . . life is so empty without you." Well, I miss you, too, mister handsome-snout. And don't worry, I'll be back in the library with you as soon as I can!

I will say Queen Moorhen's palace is quite fascinating. In my visions, it was a lot browner and damper, but in reality, it is on a lake and full of sunlight and blanket forts. I mean, that's not exactly what they are. You know how the NightWing palace had corners where any dragon could go sit and read quietly? The blanket forts are like that, but they're not for solo dragons. Each one is built for at least six dragons to curl up together, tails and talons intertwined, so they can chat about their day or share stories or make plans or just peacefully be together. There's one in nearly every room. Isn't that interesting? I haven't seen any spots for dragons to be alone — it's like they figure you'll always want to be with someone else, so there should be room for all of you. Does that make sense?

(It made me think about our library design, actually. You and I think like NightWings — well, sort of! NightWings who grew up in a really weird way! But maybe we should ask the students for ideas about study spaces. We should definitely have a blanket fort or two for our MudWings to study in together.)

Anyway anyway! I talked to Queen Moorhen, like you asked! She was very nice (just like my visions predicted!) and only a little bit completely intimidating (not sure why that wasn't in my visions!). I asked her for scrolls that would represent the most important bits of MudWing history or culture, and she took me to the palace library. (You. Would. DIE! It is SO COOL!)

She chose two scrolls and let me copy them out for you — I'm sending them along with the messenger who's bringing you this letter. I hope they're what you were looking for! The first one is the most ancient scroll they have, which is why it's all faded and in fragments. It looks like it's part of a dragon's diary and it's all about this hatching where there was a — well, you'll see! I don't want to ruin the surprise!

And then the other one is about this huge MudWing crisis a couple of centuries ago, and it's written by Queen Moorhen's own great-great-grandfather. WHAT! I wish I could be there to see your face when you get this (but in my visions you are freaking out and hugging all the scrolls you can reach).

Write back soon and let me know that you love the scrolls and also tell me everything that's happening at the school so I don't miss a single thing while I'm off on my awesome research adventure!

Love,
Fatespeaker

THE MYSTERIOUS EGG

wasn't sure what to do. It's my first hatching and I'm so afraid I did something wrong.

I know I'm supposed to just leave them. My sibs keep telling me the eggs will be fine. They're *supposed* to be alone. The nest is well sheltered and hidden by rocks, and the warm mud will protect it.

But my brothers and sisters didn't see the weird egg.

Why is it that color? What if something is wrong with the whole hatching?

I mean, it's REALLY red, like the time Taupe's tail got bitten by a hippo and it bled all over. That's not a normal egg color! What if that means the dragon inside is evil or sick or something?

Should I tell someone? What should I do?

⚶••⚶

I went back to the nest last night. I couldn't help it. I kept thinking about that red egg and I figured it would be all right to sit with the eggs for a while. It's not like the dragons inside will ever know!

I made a fire to keep warm and stared at the eggs. Seven of them, just like my sib group. I wonder if they'll be like us in any other way. I hope they have a great bigwings, like ours. But what if the red egg has the bigwings inside it? What if that color means the dragon inside is awfully sick or cold or too hot and needs help? What would happen to the rest of the dragonets if there was something wrong with the bigwings?

It probably isn't the bigwings; two of the other (normal) eggs are quite a bit bigger than it. But once I started thinking about it, I couldn't stop myself from picking up the red egg. I just wanted to see if I could feel or hear anything moving inside, and to check the temperature of the shell.

It felt normal in my talons. I mean, I don't know, I don't ever hold dragon eggs, so how would I know? But I touched the other eggs and they all felt the same. No movement, but warm and alive-feeling, I think.

I held the red egg close to the fire so I could look at the color again — and then a noise from the shadows startled me, so I jumped. The egg slipped between my claws and landed right in the fire, knocking aside some of the kindling. I yelped and burned myself getting it out.

But the egg was fine! The shell wasn't even hot. No scorch marks or anything. It's the strangest thing. I put it back in the nest and came home.

⊰✸⊱

I didn't think any of my sibs noticed when I slipped out the other night to check on the eggs, but when I got up to go again tonight, Taupe was wide-awake and waiting for me outside the sleephouse, claws crossed and tail tapping.

I told her I was just getting a little fresh air but she gave me that bigwings look, and I ended up confessing everything.

She tried to make her face look normal, but I saw the flash of alarm in her eyes. "Red?" she echoed. "Are you sure? A red egg?" She plucked a stray leaf off the wall of our house and shredded it between her claws as I told her yes, definitely, it was absolutely red.

"Show me," she said finally, so I did. We both stood around the nest staring at it, and eventually the others found us there.

"Oooorgh." Warthog wrinkled his snout at it. "Moccasin, what did you *do* to that egg? Roll it in blood?"

"Don't be gross," Taupe scolded him. She turned to me. "Moccasin, listen. My last hatching had a red egg in it, too."

"WHAAAAAAAT," said Warthog helpfully.

"And what happened?" I whispered, afraid of the look in her eyes. "Did the dragonet turn out all right?"

"No," she said. "That is — I don't know what —" She stopped and took a breath. "I sent a message to the queen about it, and she wrote back that we should destroy it."

"And you *did*?" I gasped.

"I follow orders," she said. "But this is *your* egg. If we don't tell her about it, she can't order you to destroy it. So, you decide. What do you want to do?"

I touched the red shell lightly with one claw. "I think . . . I want to let it hatch," I said.

Taupe nodded. "We'll keep an eye on it," she said. "It might be one of those fire-scales dragons that sometimes pop up in the SkyWing tribe." She eyed me for a moment. "You didn't . . . these didn't come from a SkyWing, did they?"

"No!" I said. "I don't think so." It had been dark the night of the egg-making, but I was pretty sure a SkyWing would smell different than a MudWing, right?

"Then let's cover it back up with mud," Taupe said, "and see what happens."

We were all there for the hatching today. Taupe made us hide in the boulders so the dragonets wouldn't see us. She said we might mess up their bonding if they got curious about us. I know she's our bigwings, but I have no idea how she knows all the things she does!

The bigwings in my hatching is a gigantic little dragon with a really funny bossy expression all the time. He poke-poked his way out into the world and then started helping the others out. I must admit I held my breath when he came to the red egg. What if the thing inside attacked him? Or what if it was a firescales, and it burned him?

But out came a tiny brown-gold dragonet, no different from any other newborn I've ever seen. She bonked her head into her brother's snout, giggled, and then rolled around in the mud of the nest with the others, getting totally covered. By the time all the baby dragons were hatched, I couldn't even tell which one was from the red egg.

"She seems all right," I whispered to Taupe. "Normal. Right?"

"Bit scrawny," Warthog offered. "Like you." He grinned at me.

"Normal." Taupe nodded. "That's a relief." She looked thoughtful for a moment. "We should let other dragons know somehow. So they don't get rid of any other blood-red eggs." She tapped my nose gently with her tail. "I'll find a way."

❦

I've been spying on my dragonets. Taupe would be mad, but . . . I just wanted to see if the red-egg dragon was still all right.

Which is how I saw what happened today. The little dragons were playing too close to one of the older troops, who were training and didn't notice them. I think my dragonets were pretending to be the older dragons — marching and hopping and kicking and making these cute little fight movements just like the bigger group.

But then one of the big dragons breathed out a blast of flame. She was aiming for a straw target dummy, but she was moving so fast she didn't see that one of the little dragonets was in the way.

The little red-egg baby did, though. She leaped to push her brother out of the way, and the fire caught her all along one of her wings.

I screamed, and so did a few of the MudWings in the troop. They got to her first and it was a mess of confusion and chaos and mud everywhere, so by the time I ran over, it was hard to tell what had happened, exactly. Except: there was the red-egg dragonet who'd been caught in the fire. And she was fine. Absolutely, completely fine. The burn marks faded before our eyes and she shook out her wings and gave the whole crowd of dragons a sweet, bewildered look.

All I could think was: three moons, I hatched some kind of magic baby!

There's no way to keep it secret from the queen when that many dragons saw it — but I think it will be all right. I think she will be pleased to know that MudWings might have a new power now. Maybe one day all our eggs will be red, and all our scales will be invulnerable to fire. Wouldn't that be amazing, if it all started with my egg? I wonder if my next hatching will

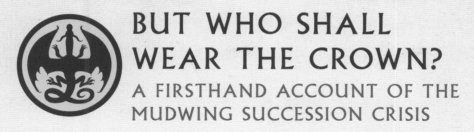

BUT WHO SHALL WEAR THE CROWN?
A FIRSTHAND ACCOUNT OF THE MUDWING SUCCESSION CRISIS

BY PRINCE SAWGRASS OF THE MUDWINGS

There were five of us, to begin with.

Three brothers, two sisters, which should have been enough.

Egret was our bigwings and destined to be the next queen of the MudWings. Royal eggs are not treated like regular MudWing eggs. We were not left to hatch in the marsh on our own. We did not have to fend for ourselves, just five siblings against the world.

Instead, we hatched in the warm underbelly of the MudWing palace, inside the mud walls of the Royal Hatchery. My first memory is Egret's claws peeling back the shell of my egg and tugging me into the chirping, whispering world. She was not that much bigger than I was, but her bigwings instincts were powerful.

The only light came from an orange sunset glowing through a hole that looked out over the lake, but it was still brighter than I'd ever known, and I blinked and blinked, wishing I could burrow back into the darkness and safety of my shell.

Three enormous dragons sat by the doorway, watching us. They did not move as Egret freed her siblings, one by one, and we kicked off the last glommy bits of egg-shell. They did whisper to one another, but we didn't understand what they were saying. We certainly didn't know that the biggest one was our mother, Anhinga, the MudWing queen. That wouldn't have meant anything to us.

We only cared about Egret's talons, Egret's warm brown eyes, Egret's strong snout nudging us all closer together. We huddled as she scooped out a nest in the mud where we could all curl up safely. We ate the worms she found for us and fell asleep, exhausted from the effort of hatching.

A normal MudWing sib group would hatch near a village and soon find their way to the older dragons nearby. Most villages have a school where young dragonets can learn the MudWing language, although many pick up the words and ways of MudWing life by following an older group around. In the palace, however, education and training begin early, and the ritual of choosing our names happens before the next full moon.

Copperhead, the smallest of us, sharp and quick. Possum, quiet and cuddly and unaccountably sad most of the time. Bayou, the other sister, the backup heir. Egret, the next queen.

And me, Sawgrass, the brother who worried.

I worried about whether there would be enough worms and roots and grubs for us to eat. I worried about the tall dragons who poked their heads in to stare at us night and day — what did they want? Who were they? Why did they keep taking our bigwings away and bringing her back and taking her away again? I worried about wrapping my mouth around the language of dragons and I worried about the weird yowling sounds of the birds on the lake and I worried about the sun going away and the strangeness of the dark and the noises of the insects and whether the sun would ever come back and then, when it did, I worried about how long we would have before it abandoned us again.

So, as you can imagine, when I was taught about how succession worked in a royal family, I worried about that a *lot*.

And, as you can perhaps also imagine, my siblings did not take my worrying very seriously.

"But this can't be right," I said to my tutor for the hundredth time. "Egret has to defeat our mother in battle to become queen? She has to . . . has to actually . . . with her own . . ."

"Yes," he said impatiently. "Princess Egret will have to kill Queen Anhinga at some point, when it is her turn to be queen."

"Unless Anhinga wins," I said, and Possum frowned at me across the classroom.

"Then we'll know Egret wasn't ready," said our tutor, "and Princess Bayou will become the heir instead."

I had nightmares about this for *years*, if you're wondering. And I think Bayou did, too, although she wouldn't admit it. She was not interested in being queen, to put it mildly. She liked *having* a bigwings; she would never want to *be* one.

"Why would Anhinga leave Egret and Bayou alive?" I asked our tutor on a different day. "If she knows one of them might — I mean, probably *will* kill her one day? Isn't she scared of them?"

He looked at me as though I'd just sneezed bullfrog guts out my nose. "The queen is not *scared* of her own dragonets," he said with polite revulsion. "She knows that heirs are necessary for a safe and well-ordered tribe. And," he added as an afterthought, "she has no sisters or nieces to take over if something should happen to her. Her hatching contained only two brothers, both of whom died in skirmishes with SkyWings before having any offspring of their own." He flicked his tail at Egret and Bayou, who were playing a building game with shells and twigs. "Those two are all we've got."

So you see, that was part of the problem right there. A new thing for me to worry about. The safety of the entire tribe was a lot to rest on the narrow shoulders of two little dragonets.

Still, we should have been all right. Even though Mother had no more eggs. Even though Bayou grew more nervous, not less, as she got older. But Egret was patient, thoughtful, wise. She waited a long time before challenging Anhinga for the throne, when the queen was old and easy to defeat.

Anhinga was not particularly affectionate to any of us — that would be weird in a MudWing family. Copperhead, Possum, Bayou, Egret, and I took care of one another. We were not very sad to say good-bye to Anhinga; we were proud of our bigwings, the new Queen Egret.

I sought her out the day after she won. She was on a large rock by the lake with the royal artists, modeling her crown for a new royal portrait.

"Time to find a match!" I said, trying to sound cheerful and casual and not at all frantic with nerves. "Better have some dragonets soon, right-o?"

(Yes, I know. I sound quite ridiculous when I'm freaking out.)

Egret rolled her eyes at me. "I've been queen for ONE DAY," she said with a laugh. "There's *plenty* of time for dragonets, you flappity tadpole."

"Yes," I said, "but, you know, still a good idea, might as well get started, very sensible, yes."

"Ugh, Sawgrass." She shoved me good-naturedly into the lake. When I came up, sputtering and with dripping weeds stuck all over my snout, she laughed again and said, "I'm happy with my sibs, I don't *want* any dragonets yet, and I don't even want to *hear* about this again for at least ten years."

"Ten *years*?" I yelped, but she had already flown away.

Still, we should have been all right. Egret was young enough and healthy, and we weren't at war with anyone. And we had Bayou, if anything happened.

"Or *you* could have dragonets, if you're really worried," Copperhead pointed out, jabbing me in the ribs with his tail.

"Me?" I said, alarmed.

I did not like talking to strangers. I never attended royal balls or conversation parties or swimming races on the lake. I had my four siblings, and they were my everything. I could not *imagine* meeting someone new or having dragonets. Would I have to become one of those large faces poking my nose into the Royal Hatchery every day? What if I had to *talk* to my dragonets? I shivered.

"Maybe *you* could?" I said hopefully to Copperhead. "Or Possum?"

He shook his head. "I never want dragonets," he said. "And Possum isn't any braver than you are. Egret will get around to it eventually, though. Just stop worrying."

He might as well have told the lake to stop being wet. I had headaches all the time and I woke up a thousand times a night in a terrible fret, but nothing I said made any difference to Egret. She had her plans, and she would not let me hurry her.

I did try, once, to meet a stranger. There was a sibling group who worked construction on the palace and the homes around it. They were all deft with their talons, building adobe structures that were strong and elegant. Sometimes I would bring out my drawing materials so I could sit and watch them work, but not because they were talented. I found them interesting because they were so calm.

I never saw them fight, nor even argue. I never saw even one of them study the clouds with anxious eyes; they never hurried or tripped or fidgeted. Their bigwings was named Olive, and she was the most serene dragon I'd ever seen.

Perhaps I should confess something here. Egret was brilliant — a wonderful queen, an amazing sister. But she was, perhaps . . . not always gentle with us. She liked to leap out of shadows and frighten us. When we were little, she liked to gather us into dark corners and tell us horror stories. Sometimes I would wake up and find her whispering scary nothings into my ear so she could giggle at the look on my face.

I don't think it was malevolent; she loved us. But she was careless with us. I think perhaps it's not entirely surprising that I worried so much, that Bayou was afraid of the crown, that Possum was quietly sad, and that Copperhead, the clever one, eventually ran away. (Although . . . with a *RainWing*? That *was* quite a shock.)

Anyway. I wondered what it would be like to have a bigwings as calm as Olive, who radiated that tranquil certainty like a blanket around her sibs.

All right, I didn't actually try to meet her. She spoke to me first.

"Prince Sawgrass, right?" she called, and I somehow managed to drop my charcoal stick, rip my papyrus, and step on my own tail all at once.

"Um," I answered.

"Can you come hold this for a moment?" She beckoned me with her tail; her talons were occupied with pressing down a mud brick.

I awkwardly joined her, awkwardly followed her instructions, awkwardly mumbled and nodded at everything she said. I don't know quite what I was doing; I was too alarmed to store much of a memory beyond my own awkwardness. But at the end, she tapped my wing with hers and said "thanks" and smiled, and that was the most conversation I had with a dragon outside my sib group or servants for probably years.

Maybe that's why I thought of her when everything fell apart.

It started with Copperhead leaving. Egret was *furious*; I mean, we all felt betrayed. How could he choose another dragon, any dragon, over us? No matter how handsome that RainWing was, he was still a *RainWing*.

Egret started asking us every day if we were loyal to her. If we would ever do that to her. She would tell us terrible stories in the dark about all the things that might happen to Copperhead, off in the rainforest with no siblings to protect him. She was a little bit meaner, a little bit more paranoid, and a lot more reckless.

You don't need all the details of how she died; I'll just tell you that she was showing off, trying to scare me (and succeeding). She always flew like the mountains would get out of *her* way, and this time, they didn't.

We all went to pieces, but nobody so much as Bayou. She cried for days, refused to eat, refused to even look at the crown, and then, she vanished. *Vanished*. The *only remaining heir* to the MudWing throne, just . . . gone, in the middle of the night.

Possum and I weren't the only ones panicking then. The entire tribe was suddenly living through my worst nightmare. Who could be queen? How would we decide? Who would rule in the meanwhile? Other tribes attacked us, stealing back hard-won territory, stealing prey and treasure, knowing we would be lost with no one in charge.

We searched further and further out on the family tree, but two generations of queens with no sisters had left us with not very many branches to stand on. There was even some muttering that Possum or I should . . . but no male dragon had ruled a tribe since the time of the Scorching. How could we start now — how could we start with one of *us*, the least kingly of all dragons?

So. You think you've guessed what happened next, don't you? You think it's what everyone else thinks: that I chose Olive, and we had dragonets, and she ruled until our daughter was old enough to be queen, and then she stepped aside to give Coypu the throne, and was the first queen in MudWing history to die peacefully of old age, with me right beside her the whole time.

Well. You're partly right. It's been long enough now that I can tell the truth, here in my final days. Coypu's granddaughter is too beloved a queen to be endangered by this information in any way.

Olive found me in the throne room, a month into the succession crisis. I was holding the crown — staring at it, really, wishing it could tell me what to do and where it belonged.

"Prince Sawgrass," she said, in her straightforward, peaceful way. "I have an idea."

"Oh?" I said, rubbing my eyes. "Um?" (My conversational skills had not improved after a month of wild-eyed MudWings yelling at me.)

"You need a queen and a royal heir," Olive said. "I have six eggs due to hatch in a few moons' time. Tell everyone they're yours and that a queen will hatch soon enough. Put me in charge in the meanwhile."

I stared at her.

"I am a great bigwings," she said calmly. "I will be a great queen. And I will take care of you."

Reader, MudWing stories are not usually full of great loves or starry-eyed romance. We leave that to the SeaWings or the SandWings. But I don't mind telling you that I fell quite a bit in love with Olive at that moment.

And you know what? She was a great queen. And so was Coypu, my adopted daughter. It may be a new royal family tree, but it is a stronger one.

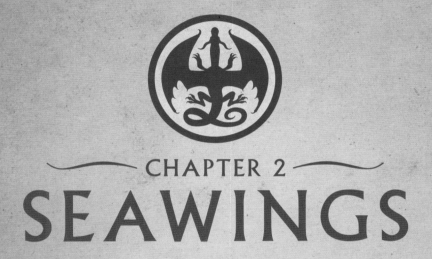

CHAPTER 2
SEAWINGS

QUEEN CORAL
IN AUKLET'S BUBBLE GARDEN

Ruins of the
Summer Palace

Kingdom of
the Sea

The Deep Palace

Bay of a Thousand Scales

SEAWINGS

SCALES: blue or green or aquamarine scales, sometimes shades of gray

EYES: green or blue

UNUSUAL CHARACTERISTICS: webs between their claws; gills on their necks; glow-in-the-dark stripes on their tails/snouts/underbellies

ABILITIES: can breathe underwater; see in the dark; create huge waves with one splash of their powerful tails; excellent swimmers

HABITAT: the shallow seas and the archipelago around the Bay of a Thousand Scales

DIET: fish, whales, octopuses, clams, sea birds

QUEEN: Queen Coral

Dear Starflight,

Thank you for your charming letter with all the updates about Anemone and Turtle and their classes. I must say I expected Tsunami to be a better correspondent. I cannot believe she inherited so little of my writerly talent or inclination!

I mean, what is the use of having one daughter there to keep a close eye on my other daughter if she doesn't immediately transmit every single observation back to me in exacting detail? How am I supposed to go through my days without knowing what Anemone is doing every single moment? My BABY?

I am sure Tsunami cannot be that busy. It is only a school, not an entire kingdom, after all. Do give her a series of stern nudges for me, will you?

In any case, I was thrilled to receive your request for more scrolls! DO I have scrolls!! You can stop writing to the other kingdoms at once; I can fill your entire library with my oeuvre alone! Oh, your lucky students! This is so marvelous!

Your letter inspired my creative muse and I was up all night writing a brand-new scroll for your library. You asked for history, and what could be more important than my (and of course the SeaWing tribe's) essential role in ending the Great War?

As soon as I finished, I woke up a scribe so she could make several copies. Yours is the very second, or maybe the third. You'll see I've inscribed it to your library myself, with my signature, of course, so this is now quite a valuable item.

I am also enclosing a complete list of my works, with brief descriptions of each. Read it over and then write to my niece, Moray, to let us know which ones you'd like for the library and how many copies of each. I will make sure she gives you our friends-and-family discount!

Moray has just pointed out that you asked for scrolls of ancient SeaWing history by dragons who are not *me, and I retorted that you certainly did not put it that way, and* she responded that it was *implied even though she agrees that scrolls by dragons who are* not *me could not* possibly *be as interesting or valuable to your little guide as scrolls* by me. But *since she is being quite a sea cucumber about it, I will let her send you copies of some letters we found from Queen Lagoon and Albatross, written before the Massacre. I trust that will be quite sufficient and anything else you need, you can find in the scrolls* I have written.

Auklet sends her love to Tsunami and Anemone and Turtle, and we both hope they will come home for a visit again soon! Perhaps for my next reading! I might even dedicate this newest scroll to Tsunami, but don't tell her that—let's have it be a wonderful surprise! *(Unless her next letter is as disappointingly bland as the last three, in which case perhaps I will dedicate this scroll to you, Starflight, instead, and serve her right.)*

— Coral, Queen of the SeaWings

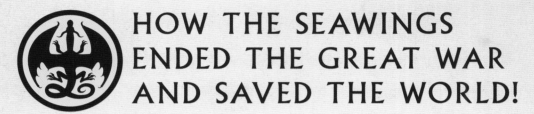

HOW THE SEAWINGS ENDED THE GREAT WAR AND SAVED THE WORLD!

BY QUEEN CORAL OF THE SEAWINGS

Once upon a time, there was an absolutely dreadful war started by a trio of squabbling SandWing sisters.

The oldest sister, Burn, was *alarmingly* grumpy, mean, terrifying, and violent. She was obsessed with weird, creepy things and she loved war. She would *clearly* have been a terrible queen!

And yet, because she was so big and scary and brutal, not to mention the oldest sister, she nearly took the throne the moment her mother died. In fact, she probably would have easily won the war in the first year . . . were it not for the brave and fearless SeaWings!

You see, the SandWing sisters knew they needed allies to help them fight. So Burn came to Queen Coral of the SeaWings and *demanded* her assistance. She said if the SeaWings didn't help her, she'd bring her army to wipe them out! She'd bring the SkyWings, too! She'd rain fire from the skies!

But none of this frightened Queen Coral or her courageous council. They knew Burn was a menace who must be stopped! They also knew they could withstand the entire SandWing army and all the SkyWings as well! And also that the SeaWing palaces were well hidden and ha ha ha to any fire-breathing tribes who tried to find them! Good luck, sand-snorters!

The SeaWings also received a message from the youngest sister, Blaze. She had fled to the outskirts of the Ice Kingdom and was hiding under the wing of Queen Glacier.

Queen Coral could tell from the moment she received the letter that this was not the ally for her. Blaze could *barely* spell or string a sentence together, and it was *abundantly* clear from her missive that this SandWing had never read a *single one* of Queen Coral's bestselling scrolls. Possibly she did not even know that Queen Coral was a bestselling author! Possibly she had never read a scroll in her life!

Well, Queen Coral knew that she could not curse the SandWings with such an ignorant queen. Nor could she leave them to the mercy of the menacing Burn, who *also*, by the way, clearly had no interest in scrolls, and only ever referred to Queen Coral's bestsellers in a dismissive, some might even say *smirking*, way.

No, no! There was only one potential SandWing queen who could be a suitable ally for the SeaWings. She was clever and charming. She came bearing ingenious battle plans and mountains of treasure to pay our SeaWing soldiers. Most important, she had read *all* of Queen Coral's scrolls, and could *quote them at length* or refer to their plots from memory. She thought Queen Coral was a *brilliant* writer. She was exceptionally intelligent and discerning, and her name was Blister.

At first, the MudWings were in the alliance with Blister and the SeaWings — but after they betrayed us most perniciously by assassinating our beloved Commander Tempest, Blister executed their top general and the offending guards. She held true to the SeaWing alliance, accepted a hidden base for her SandWings on one of our islands, and continued to lavish treasure and support on Queen Coral and her loyal tribe.

All seemed well. The SeaWings had clearly chosen the right sister to support; they were destined to win the war and become the most powerful allied tribes in all the kingdoms!

But in the final year of the war, a strange twist of fate revealed a dark side to Blister.

It all began with the arrival of Queen Coral's long-lost daughter, the missing princess herself (see *The Missing Princess*, by Queen Coral), a dragonet named Tsunami. Tsunami had inherited her mother's courage and determination, but not, unfortunately, her elegance, grace, or communication skills. Nonetheless, she had become the leader of a little ragtag group of dragonets who were supposed to be part of a prophecy (which, mind you, would have been a much better written, clearer prophecy if *I* had written it!).

They arrived in the Kingdom of the Sea like a hurricane swooping across the ocean. Within days of their arrival, Tsunami had uncovered a murder plot years in the making and saved the newest princess, an absolute perfect angel darling of a dragon named Auklet. But along with this wondrous turn of events came chaos and destruction: (1) the arrival of a traitor who had gone missing, named Webs; (2) the mysterious death of Queen Coral's most trusted advisor, Whirlpool; and (3) a vicious and catastrophic attack by the SkyWings that resulted in the fall of the Summer Palace itself!

Through all this, it became apparent that Blister might not be as trustworthy as she seemed (*despite* her quality taste in literature!). Possibly she murdered a SkyWing in our territory and lied to me about it? Potentially she was conspiring with NightWings? Perhaps she was trying to get us to mistrust and lock up the dragonets including Tsunami? *Maaaaybe* she was actually just manipulating everyone and had her own sinister agenda all along? It was all very confusing!

Faced with this mysterious turn of events, the valiant queen and her council retreated to the Deep Palace. They knew that the most helpful, brave, and useful thing they could do was to stay in seclusion until Tsunami and her subordinates figured out how to end the war. They sensed that Tsunami had a plan — a plan no doubt forged in the crucible of her experience in the Kingdom of the Sea!

Merely a few days in the company of the queen and her council had added years of wisdom to the brain of this young princess! She had learned so much from her mother (and her mother's scrolls, and her lessons with poor, fallen Whirlpool) in such a short time. She was ready to go forth and bring an end to the war, if only the queen and the rest of the SeaWing tribe could buy her enough time with some extremely valiant hiding.

And so the SeaWings separated themselves from Blister and weakened her in the crucial final days of the war. And *that* is why, in the end, all the terrible sisters were defeated, and the war came to a close, and the dragons of Pyrrhia lived happily ever after.

(There are some scurrilous alternate versions of this truth being spread about by a few spiteful NightWings and SandWings. Do not listen to them! There was a plan all along and Queen Coral was definitely in on it!)

A BRIEF SUMMARY OF SOME OF THE GREATEST SCROLLS OF ALL TIME BY THE MOST WORLD-RENOWNED SEAWING AUTHOR IN THE HISTORY OF PYRRHIA, QUEEN CORAL

THE MISSING PRINCESS: The #1 bestselling scroll in the ocean, this heart-wrenching tale of a princess kidnapped from her rightful family and their valiant, awe-inspiring quest to find her has now been updated with an interview between the author and the real-life missing princess herself!

THE CLAWS OF MURDER: A dark secret haunts this noble SeaWing family. A cunning murderer hides within their midst. One stalwart detective is on the case: Is it her sleepy-eyed father? Her cackling brother? Her handsome assistant? Follow the clues straight into . . . THE CLAWS OF MURRRRRRDERRRRRRR!

THE SINISTER JELLYFISH: When a talking jellyfish arrives in the court of the SeaWing queen, it is welcomed as a magical miracle . . . until it starts spreading malicious gossip about the princesses. What is this jellyfish up to? What does it want? WHY IS IT SO SINISTER AND WHO IS GOING TO EAT IT FIRST?

A TAIL OF BLOOD: Our brave detective returns in the wake of the shattering events of *The Claws of Murder* to discover that YET ANOTHER MURRRRRRRDERER is lurking in the heart of her family! Who is it this time? Surely not the handsome assistant! He's so handsome! And he adores her so much! Or could it be . . . a conspiracy of jealous siblings? Only one thing is certain: BLOODSHED!

THE VERY GREEDY SCAVENGER: Queen Coral's dazzling debut foray into the realm of scrolls for dragonets! This cautionary tale of a small, squishy scavenger who can't stop stealing from dragons will keep your little ones in giggly suspense all the way to the delightfully happy ending, when the scavenger is finally captured and eaten by a clever little SeaWing.

THE PUDDLE THAT DREAMED OF BECOMING AN OCEAN: A brilliant rumination on purpose, destiny, ambition, quashing silly ideas, knowing your place, the true wetness of your soul, and making a splash!

ALL HAIL THE SQUID OF DESTINY: The first book in this epic fantasy saga about a trio of sentient squids and their grand adventures under the sea — told from the point of view of the squids themselves! Will they band together to save their world from a dark and ancient kraken, or will the forces of fate wind evil tentacles around THEIR VERY SOULS?

BITE, SWIM, ROAR: Queen Coral's travel memoir about all her royal visits to the kingdoms around Pyrrhia, full of glorious detail, wise inner thoughts, and clever observations about the very weird habits of other tribes.

ONE MOON, TWO MOON, THREE MOONS: A sweet counting book for your littlest dragonets.

WHEN WE SWAM THE OCEAN DEEP and THE ISLAND AT THE BEGINNING OF TIME: Do not miss this riveting two-part historical adventure about some of the earliest dragon settlers in the Bay of a Thousand Scales! This ornately detailed family drama imagines court life in the days of the first SeaWing queens after the Scorching, including how they built the Deep Palace, the dragons they loved, the dragons they murdered, and how one princess clawed her way over her sisters to ultimate power.

I'm afraid including the complete catalog of Queen Coral's works would have occupied the entire rest of this guide, so I am presenting just the first ten on her list, and hoping she will forgive me eventually!
— Starflight

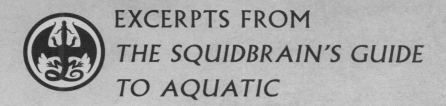

EXCERPTS FROM
THE SQUIDBRAIN'S GUIDE
TO AQUATIC

Now that the tribes are spending a lot more time together (thanks, dragonets of destiny!) all you non-SeaWings may have noticed that your new SeaWing friends sometimes flash their scales and make a lot of talon gestures while they're talking to one another. Maybe you've even noticed one SeaWing start laughing while another tries to look totally serious, and when you asked them what the joke was, they both said "Nothing!" really fast.

Well, those flashes? They're part of the awesome SeaWing language of Aquatic, used by SeaWings since even before the Scorching to talk to one another underwater.

We can't teach you everything (*your* scales can't flash, and only SeaWings can truly speak Aquatic, after all!), but we figured we'd help you out a little bit. If you study and pay attention, hopefully this scroll will help you understand your SeaWing friends a little better!

QUESTION SCALES

The flashing scales on a dragon's snout are known as "question" scales and are added to other scale patterns to create questions. Specifically, they can be used to say words like:

- Who? (short flash)
- What? (two flashes)
- Where? (three flashes of three different snout scales)
- How? (long flash)
- When? (short flash followed by long flash)
- Why? (triple flash)

INSULTS

A particular favorite of dragonets is a certain tail stripe frequently used as "insult" scales. Dragons use these stripes (and usually some talon gestures) to say exactly what they think about each other — or about you, behind your back! Common SeaWing insults include:

- Squid-brain (three flashes)
- Sea urchin up his snout (one long flash)
- Shark bait (two short flashes and a flick of the talons)
- Creeping tentacle (one quick flash with a talon wriggle)
- Stuck-up barnacle (two flashes with talons tapped together and pointed upward)
- Moon eel (two quick flashes and draw a circle with a talon)
- Sponge-snout (one long flash with a talon wriggle)

SWOONY STUFF

Sometimes we SeaWings need to express affection, and the only way to do so is by flashing our scales and flapping our talons. Some SeaWings are extremely sappy in Aquatic in a way they would never be in Dragon! Most of these involve the scales along a dragon's sides — close to their heart! Some phrases to use on a crush:

- My sweet seashell (two short flashes with a talon on your heart)
- Ocean's delight (one short flash with a talon on your heart)
- Adorable sea turtle (one long flash while bringing talons together)
- Beloved dolphin of my heart (two short flashes with talons crossed across chest)
- Sparkling teeth (three flickers and a tail tap)

COMMON EXPRESSIONS

There are certain phrases most SeaWings use frequently. Some are only spoken in Dragon, some are only presented in Aquatic, and some are common to both languages. They involve many different scales and talon gestures. Here are a few of my favorites:

- Three moons! (all snout scales flash three times)
- Like sand through my talons (quick flash of side stripes with talons outstretched and wriggling)
- Snapper got your tail? (tail scales flicker while tail whips back and forth)
- You look like you've been shocked by an eel! (all scales flashing rapidly, talons shaking wildly)

Albatross,

I've been very patient, haven't I, all these years? Your work has taken much longer than you promised, but I have waited because you vowed it would be spectacular. I've left you to your projects in peace since the tragic death of your wife.

But you've taken things too far with the animus tests, holding them so rarely and complaining so much. From now on, each year you'll test all two-year-old dragonets and anyone else I tell you to test. We'll hold the next test next month, and we'll make sure your granddaughter and grandson are tested. We'll have no more Sapphires.

In the meantime, I want a scroll from you on the methods you'll use to hold the test going forward and what you've done in the past. Have it to me by tomorrow morning.

— Queen Lagoon

Lagoon,

    As I'm sure you remember, your first animus test was unsuccessful. In fact, all your tests have been unsuccessful because there are no animus dragons in this tribe besides me.

    But your tests have also been stupidly conceived and executed. For instance, at the first, you suggested that each dragon present command the water to turn to ice. All the dragons spoke at once, so if one of them had been an animus dragon, we wouldn't have known whose spell worked.

    And if one of them had been magical, it could have been a catastrophic disaster. Given the language you used, it's quite likely that I, a grown animus dragon in full possession of my powers, would have frozen the ocean as far as the Deep Palace with that spell. The damage would have been remarkable. Imagine what an untried dragonet might have done.

    For the next ridiculous "test," you commanded me to perform a display of magic that would "inspire" a young animus. Half the dragonets were so scared that they dropped the shells they were meant to enchant and dove into the ocean. At least one was never seen again.

    Every exam you've commanded has been a mess like this. If you continue to insist on this unnecessary exercise, next time I suggest we use coconuts. I'll tell the dragonets to command the coconut to fly or roll or bounce, one at a time. No fuss, and it'll quickly be clear how powerless they all are.

    I am your one and only animus dragon, and eventually you are going to have to accept that.

— Albatross

My dear *Albatross*,

I'm certain that when I asked you to impress our dragonets with a magnificent light show, I didn't tell you to light all the trees on fire and shoot sparks and flames at the crowd until they fled in terror to avoid being burned to death on the beach. I'm also sure that you laughing at them as they fled contributed to the fact that two of those dragons still have nightmares. Or maybe it was the seagulls that dropped out of the air due to the smoke and then came back to life, only to dive-bomb the dragonets who dared poke their heads above water?

You really shouldn't blame me for your mistakes, Albatross. I am your one and only queen, after all.

I look forward to our next trial, when I know your coconut test will produce the result I want. I'd hate for you to feel burdened by your work as my animus and your duty to our tribe. When I find my next animus, I'll make sure that they're trained quickly and maybe I won't need you anymore. I'm sure you would enjoy a long, quiet rest, away from the tribe.

Next month, Albatross, you better get this right.

— Queen Lagoon

Hi Starflight!

*I'm afraid I missed your deadline to write up a scroll about SeaWing traditions —
I mean, I did swim to the literal other side of the world recently, so I kind of thought that
might earn me a pass on some of the homework!*

*But since it's for your book, I thought maybe you could use this letter. It's from one of
my (many) brothers, Fin, inviting me to our hatching day party this year. We've always
had to throw our own parties, since Mother was so busy with being queen and fighting a
war and trying to keep a princess alive. And no one really expected much else of us,
so several of my brothers are basically party-throwing experts.*

*I'd invite you or Kinkajou or Peril to join us, but a lot of it will be underwater, so it
won't be much fun for non-SeaWings. Kinkajou said maybe we can have a Jade Mountain
hatching day party for me when I get back, and then Peril offered to set a cake on fire for
me, which I did NOT know was a thing! Do all the tribes with fire set their hatching day
cakes aflame to celebrate? It seems like rather a waste of a cake! Do you still eat the
scorched crumbs? Tribes with fire are weird. Sensible dragons know that the best hatching
day food is raw tuna wrapped in seaweed and stuffed with little fish eggs. YUM.*

— Turtle

TURTLE, you ABSOLUTE MOLLUSK,

Mother said there's a chance you won't be coming home next month for our hatching day party, and that is NOT ACCEPTABLE, little brother!

Yes, yes, I know fancy hugging school takes up all your time. (Who knew learning to hug and <u>understand each other</u> would be so time-consuming?) And occasionally you also have to fight enormous ancient bad guys from thousands of years ago, and blah blah something about animus powers and Anemone and whatever, but! Turtle! HATCHING DAY PARTY!

It just won't be the same if there are only thirty-one of us! Well, OK, considering that you usually sit in a corner and read a scroll and fall asleep way before the rest of us, maybe it'll be basically the same. But YOU will miss US. Can you imagine having a QUIET hatching day? I'm sure not even an extremely cute rainbow-colored RainWing can make up for all thirty-one of your brothers! (Ha ha, yes, I heard some excellent gossip. A RainWing! You hilarious manatee. Only you could manage to fall for someone even sleepier than you!)

Listen, this is going to be the best hatching day party we've ever had. You can't miss it! Mother even said she would come and do a special reading of her next book, so . . . yay? But that does mean literally EVERYONE who's anyone will be there (like, by royal command, but we can make sure they also have fun!).

We'll be having our traditional hatching day triathlon — I know swimming and flying and running aren't all your favorite things, but you can come cheer for me while I beat the snouts off Cerulean and Octopus! And of course we'll have our usual treasure hunt through the islands for actual buried treasure, which you have mysteriously won WAY too many times. Plus, coral reef hide-and-seek, a humpback-whale-themed singing competition, and an ocean pet fashion show to see who has the cutest seahorses, sea dragons, or cuttlefish (It's me; wait until you meet my new bobtail squid!)

And, of course, an EPIC FEAST. Sharks for everyone! So many tuna rolls! The most legendary pile of lobsters you can imagine! Turtle, you have to come. Your super-special hugging school has brought you out of your shell too much and your taste in friends and crushes is questionable, but you're still our brother, and you fill a very important role in the established teasing order.

Write and tell me you're coming! If I don't hear back, I'm sending Octopus to hunt you down with Anemone's old harness.   — Fin

P.S. I'm sure you thought it was SO FUNNY to send us all off on that wild-whale chase to the Outer Isles with your whole freaked-out "Anemone might turn evil" thing. I took ALL OUR BROTHERS with me, Turtle! Plus some of their girlfriends and boyfriends! By the time we came slinking back, the whole palace thought we'd gone off to start our own kingdom! (Except Mother, who didn't exactly notice we were gone.) I couldn't precisely explain that we ran off to hide from our little sister. So HA HA HA, very clever prank — and payback is coming, just you wait.

P.P.S. But not at the hatching day party, I promise! Truce until it's over! Come come come!

Dear Tamarin,

I hope I am doing these bumpy letters right. It is really cool that you and Starflight invented this little letter-presser thing so we can make scrolls that blind dragons can read. I hope it works, because I want to write you some notes that are JUST FOR YOU and not to be read by ANY OTHER NOSY RAINWINGS WHO CLAIM TO BE HELPING BUT ARE ACTUALLY SNOOPING ON MY CORRESPONDENCE, not to name any names (KINKAJOU).

But this one is for practice, and for Starflight's peculiar book project, so I will save all the JUST FOR YOU stuff for my next letter, because I bet "Tamarin, you said the smartest thing in history yesterday, and it made me think for the whole rest of the day, and sometimes when I'm falling asleep I imagine going flying with you, and can we please have another gardening date because planting marigolds with you was the most peaceful I've ever felt in my life" is probably not what Starflight is looking for.

Did he give you this weird assignment, too? Write an essay about your tribe's strengths and weaknesses? Um, hello! SeaWings HAVE no weaknesses! What a ridiculous question! We're the best and strongest and most creative tribe! Who's written the most scrolls? SeaWings! Who has the coolest palaces? SeaWings! Who has their OWN LANGUAGE that NO OTHER TRIBE knows how to speak? THAT'S RIGHT, SEAWINGS.

Not to mention how we can breathe underwater — no one else can do that! (MudWings don't count; they are just holding their breath for a long time! Not the same!) Also, we can see in the dark, and our scales light up, and we're the best swimmers, obviously.

I think probably the only thing that isn't *the super awesomest about being a SeaWing is that I can't ever bring you home to show you the Deep Palace. That is, we're kind of off on our own, way down under the ocean. I never met anyone who wasn't a SeaWing except Blister (IMAGINE MY GRUMPIEST FACE HERE) until Tsunami brought all her friends to the Summer Palace. Some of the other dragons at Jade Mountain know lots of dragons from other tribes — they talk about places like Possibility and Sanctuary and the Scorpion Den, where all kinds of dragons hang out with one another. And sometimes that makes me just the tiniest bit jealous.*

Like . . . it would be kind of cool if there was a place like Possibility on the coast of the MudWing kingdom, don't you think? Somewhere where SeaWings, MudWings, and RainWings could all hang out together. Maybe it could have an ENORMOUS garden with ALL the plants in Pyrrhia and you and I could plant it together! And then I could take you swimming in the ocean and you could meet some dolphins, who are really funny. You will love dolphins, Tamarin.

My mother, Queen Coral, is working on rebuilding a palace where we can have visitors who aren't SeaWings. I'm not sure if it'll be the Summer Palace . . . everyone's still a little freaked out by what happened there. Some of the Council suggested reopening the Island Palace, although that's not exactly the least traumatizing location in our tribe's history either!

I'd like to have an above-water palace, I think. I mean, I'm glad we have the Deep Palace to hide in if we need to, but I'd rather be a queen who can have a RainWing friend come stay with her. I mean, hypothetically, or some other kind of friend, maybe.

I'm not sure I should be the next SeaWing queen, though. Maybe it should be Auklet instead. She hasn't made any terrible decisions yet, or ruined anyone's lives, or, say, tried to kill any family members. So I suppose *there's an argument to be made that she'd be a better queen than me. But then I could also say she is too small for us to tell what she's really like, and possibly she'll do something even worse than what I did! (Although I guess that would be hard.)*

Really I hope Mother is queen for a long long time, and I hope that I get to stay at Jade Mountain Academy for a long long long time. I just want to be myself and make my own decisions and have a normal dragonet life for a while.

And maybe that life could include some seeds and dirt and violets? I'm free tomorrow after lunch if you are!

> *Love,*
> *Anemone*

P.S. I was going to give you this pearl that I found that is cool and splodgy-looking, but certain dragons (Kinkajou) threatened me with some HIGHLY UNCALLED FOR VIOLENCE if I ever give you anything, in case it's enchanted, even though I promise I would never do that, but I guess I can see her point, so if you would like to HOLD a cool, squodgy-looking black pearl sometime, you should stop by my room (and yes, your huffy overprotective friend can come, too).

CHAPTER 3
RAINWINGS

The Indestructible City

Mud Kingdom

Queen Moorhen's Palace

RainWing Village

NightWing Village

Rainforest Kingdom

Portal to SandWing Kingdom

Portal to NightWing Island

RAINWINGS

SCALES: constantly shifting colors; usually bright, like birds-of-paradise

EYES: primarily shades of green, yellow, brown, or blue, but they appear to change based on the shifting scales around them

UNUSUAL CHARACTERISTICS: prehensile tails; scales that change color based on their emotions or intentionally for decoration or camouflage

ABILITIES: can camouflage their scales to blend into their surroundings; shoot a deadly venom from their fangs

HABITAT: the southern rainforest, east of the mountains

DIET: fruit and other rainforest plants

QUEEN: Queen Glory

Dear Queen Glory,

I hope all is well with you and your two tribes. I know how very busy you are, but I had hoped to receive your submissions weeks ago for the important guide we are creating here at the academy to teach dragons about tribes other than their own. I would hate to have the RainWing section be much shorter than the other sections.

There is so much the other tribes still don't know about RainWings and the rainforest where they live. I know you feel strongly about breaking down the negative stereotypes about your dragons, and that is precisely the mission of our project.

One possible scroll we could excerpt is Dangers of the Rainforest — you might remember it from our days under the mountain. I'm enclosing a copy here for your review in case you would like to add or change anything.

Please write and send your submissions as soon as you can.

– Starflight

P.S. I miss you.

Starflight, don't be such a melon-brain (and you know you don't have to call me Queen Glory or sound so very stuffy in your letters!). Of course I didn't forget about the VERY IMPORTANT guide to dragons that you're working on. I just have been a trifle busy, since I am, you know, the queen of TWO tribes (thanks to YOU).

Since most of our RainWings are still learning to read and write, you are now in possession of some of the only known contemporary RainWing writings in the whole world. You better treat these scrolls with the care and respect they deserve: clean claws only.

Starflight. I'm joking. I know you'd never touch a scroll with dirty claws.

The first scroll I'm sending is one you're familiar with: it is the first complete story written by a RainWing with her own claws in possibly hundreds of years. True, that RainWing is very young and the story is not exactly "polished," but I think it is a wonderful example of this tribe's potential, especially considering how hard she worked to learn to write so quickly. I am referring, of course, to Kinkajou's creative writing project. You may correct the spelling, but don't you dare change anything else about it! Kinkajou and I think it's perfect just the way it is.

I updated the Dangers of the Rainforest *scroll that you sent, which I remember was supremely UNhelpful when we first came here. It turns out the rainforest is hardly dangerous at all, especially now that we don't have a certain tribe sneaking about trying to kidnap us!*

Handsome shared what he could about the traditional contests for choosing a RainWing queen.

Oh, and I wrote down everything Jambu shared about RainWing colors and emotions — he had rather an extraordinary amount to say on this subject, so I had to limit him to his favorite and least favorite colors. (It's still a lot!)

Jokes aside, you are doing an amazing job with this collection and I can't wait to read it when it's done. And I miss you, too. Melon-brain.

Love,
Glory

THE STUPENDOUS STORY
OF A SNUGGLY SLOTH

BY KINKAJOU OF THE RAINWINGS

Once upon a time (which is actually also right now — is it weird to write a story about someone who's still alive but start it with "once upon a time"? Moon says it's all right, and she has read more scrolls than ANYONE except I guess probably Starflight, but if I ask him, I'm worried he'll say I can't and it's such a classic beginning! I really want to do it! OK, I'm doing it! It's my story! Maybe I'm being daring and literary! Maybe I'm breaking all the rules because I'm super avant-garde!) (Or maybe writers do this all the time, Moon says, although she also says they don't usually start their stories with long parenthetical (she had to spell that word for me!) asides and worries because she says mostly those stay inside the writers' heads, which is totally mystifying because isn't writing all about putting *everything* in your head onto a scroll so other dragons can understand you and know all your thoughts? Moon says no, and that probably most dragons besides me wouldn't want everyone to know ALL their thoughts, and that maybe we should have a lesson on story structure and focus but THAT SOUNDS BORING, SO), there was a very beautiful and cuddly sloth named Silver.

Silver was clever and friendly, but she was also a little bit lonely. All the other sloths thought she chirped too much and needed to sleep more and be more quiet. She had one teacher who yelled at her all the time and wouldn't answer any of her really great, useful questions. (Moon wants to know what kind of teacher a sloth could possibly have and when I said how would I know? she said I was making up the story so I could make up ANYTHING! So I said all right, the grumpy sloth was a CALCULUS teacher! And then Moon wanted to know if I had any idea what calculus was, which I thought was very rude, but then she said she didn't know what it was either, and I said it was something I heard Mastermind say in the NightWing fortress and it seemed mathy, perhaps, and Moon asked why by all the moons would a bunch of sloths be learning math? And so maybe I should make it, like, a naptime teacher or a climbing teacher instead, and I said, WHO IS TELLING THIS STORY ANYWAY? (the answer is ME!) and there's a lot going on here so stop worrying about what the teacher is teaching and think about how she is being mean to Silver because that is the actual point!)

So sometimes Silver was a little bit sad. I mean, *she* didn't think she was annoying! She just wanted to learn things and get better at stuff and be a really great sloth, and it wasn't her fault that most of the other sloths would rather be snoozing or flopping around thinking about snoozing and acted like she was just the very most exhausting sloth they'd ever met. Right?

Silver knew if she just had a chance and some training and some other slightly more energetic sloths to hang out with, she could do something awesome like save the world! (And guess what SHE WAS RIGHT!) (Moon says I can't write that because I'm spoiling the end of the story, but she doesn't know the end of the story because I haven't even written it yet so what is she even talking about? Also maybe this is another very advanced literary trick that I have invented and other authors are going to want to copy it forever! Moon says she is starting to sympathize with the exhausted sloths, like, what does that even mean?)

Silver liked to go out and wander the rainforest, hoping to meet other sloths who were more like her. (Moon says this would be a good place for some description of the scenery UGH I HATE those bits! OK, FINE.) The trees were really green. They were also very tall. Most of the time they were pretty wet because this was a RAINforest. There were loud monkeys who were nearly as cute as Silver and quiet snakes who were not cute at all. The wind went *whoosh-whoosh* and the trees smelled like wet leaves. (Is that enough scenery description?) (Moon says she is trying to write her own essay over there, in which case I ask you why she asked me to read aloud each sentence after I write it, and now she's saying she did NOT ask me to do that, which, hmmm, I don't know, I'm pretty sure I remember her saying something like that.) (She wants to know if possibly I misinterpreted the conversation where I said: "I'm going to write a story!" and she said, "That sounds great! Please do not read me each sentence out loud after you write it!" I don't think that's what happened! I think her mind reading is cluttering up her brain and she just imagined it, that's what!)

One day, Silver was exploring a part of the rainforest that was full of dragons. Some sloths said it was dangerous to go near the dragons in case they got hungry, but Silver was quite smart and had noticed that several sloths had pet dragons, so she knew that

they were really probably easy to tame and not as bitey as they looked. (Moon does not like the word *bitey*, which she says is not a real word, but if it is a word I can SAY OUT LOUD and you know EXACTLY what I mean, then how can it not be a real word, I mean, seriously.)

Silver was not sure if she wanted a pet dragon, because what if her pet dragon also thought she was annoying, and what if it maybe ran away from her? What if she was the kind of sloth who just wanted to love somebody with all her whole entire heart and express that love with great enthusiasm all the time, but she never found anybody who wanted it?

So she watched the dragons for a while. They seemed to like sleeping. There were many of them in many beautiful colors. But was one of them the dragon for her? And how could she tell?

And then suddenly a whole caboodle of new dragons arrived! (Silver did not know how many, because everyone knows that sloths cannot count beyond three.) (Moon is giving me a dubious face about this fact, so I am ignoring her.)

Most of these new dragons could not change color. There was a big, hungry brown one; a small, happy yellow one; a pretty big, loud blue one; a wounded, sad blue one;

and a super-intelligent, wise, noble, generous, brilliant black one who was clearly destined to be an excellent teacher who gives out top grades to students who work really, really hard even if their spelling is not always *exactly* totally accurate. (Moon says we are not supposed to burble compliments all over the dragons who are grading these essays, but if *I* were a teacher and *I* had to read thirty-five endless scrolls by my students (and you KNOW some of them are going to be SUPER boring!), then *I* think I would be *delighted* to come across an occasional nice and obviously true remark about myself!) (Now she is pointing out that Webs is also one of our teachers, so just in case: a wounded, sad, very fascinating, and definitely never boring blue one.)

BUT the *important* part is that there was ANOTHER dragon with them! She was one of the rainbow color-changing dragons, but she was quite a bit louder and snappier than they were. She had this shiny brilliant greatness that just radiated all around her, like maybe she had the sun inside her somewhere. When bad things happened, she didn't go back to sleep or hide her nose under some leaves or pretend it wasn't important. She jumped up and did something! She was a DOER of THINGS! And that made her different from all the sloths Silver had ever known and different from all the dragons Silver had been watching.

Like, when the other rainforest dragons shot sleeping darts at her friends, the new dragon yelled and got stompy and made them come out and explain things. And when she found out dragons were missing, she went *looking for them* even though she *didn't even know them*, unlike *literally everyone else in the village* who did know them but did nothing. Although actually that bit happened later, but Silver could probably tell she was just that kind of dragon by looking at her.

(I asked Moon if she wanted to twitch her eyebrows at me for writing nice things about my queen, too, but she just gave me this quiet, sad-thoughtful face and said no, that bit's all right, and she thinks she understands my story now. Which is so weird; Moon is so weird! It's just a story about a lonely little sloth finding a dragon who can take care of her! Three moons!)

So Silver followed the new dragon, whose name turned out to be Glory, all the way back to the rainforest village. And she watched until Glory fell asleep, and then she carefully, carefully, slowly, slowly, slowly inched her way up the dragon's shoulder. The sloth curled up in a little sunlit hollow on Glory's back, where she fit just right. And that's where she fell asleep, knowing she had found the perfect dragon, and that from now on, everything was going to be much better, and they were going to live happily ever after together.

——— THE END ———

P.S. Moon wants to know what happened to the saving-the-world part, which just goes to show you shouldn't think you can guess the end of a story! But also, obviously Silver saved the world by being such an excellent sloth friend to Glory that Glory was able to do many awesome world-saving things. It is much easier to save the world with friends who support you and love you no matter what! Also, I ran out of room on this scroll, so I figure I should end it here. (Moon says she is SHOCKED and can't imagine how that happened, like, hello, this *is* my very first story! And plus besides I have decided I am a writer who shares all the thoughts in my head plus also the conversations around me; it is a LITERARY STYLE CHOICE THING, and I think other RainWings will appreciate it, thank you very much.)

 DANGERS OF THE RAINFOREST

The rainforest of the RainWing kingdom is thought to be full of many fascinating and dangerous creatures, from poisonous snakes and deadly bugs to chattering birds and hooting monkeys. There are also strange geological features that may pose a threat, and many kinds of trees and plants that have yet to be studied in depth, so proceeding with caution in this environment is highly recommended.

The most famous of the rainforest snakes is, of course, the green anaconda. While not poisonous, this snake, which lives in and near water, can easily strangle a small dragon if she is not aware of her surroundings. The deadliest snake in Pyrrhia, the dragonbite viper, has not been seen in the rainforest, but its cousin, the lancehead, does inhabit this territory and has been known to poison prey as large as scavengers.

While many of the rainforest's deadly bugs are quite small, their venom can be lethal. From tiny wandering spiders that prowl the forest floor to the giant centipede, which injects its venom into its prey's bloodstream, these bugs are an invisible threat to all who venture into the rainforest.

There are several types of monkeys in the rainforest. Their names, if they have them, are known only to RainWings, and they are of various sizes and levels of edibility. They do not appear to be dangerous per se, but they can be *exceptionally* loud and annoying, so be prepared for that.

*Very specific and full of helpful information, this writer. To actually offer some useful notes on monkeys — there are large brown monkeys that used to make normal grunting sounds, but NOW they make screaming noises. Starflight thinks that his father, Mastermind, may have done something to them to make them scream like that. He thinks it was to scare off the MudWing soldiers that used to hang out in the rainforest, but I think it was to give RainWings awful dreams so they'd be too tired to resist when the NightWings came to take over. — **Glory***

One interesting rainforest feature is the quicksand pit. A dragon who steps into one of these will quickly sink down until sand covers her body up to her torso, keeping the dragon trapped there but not killing her.

Of the mysterious RainWings, not much is known. They seem to be a peaceful, lazy tribe that prefers to lounge in the sunshine, and they have no interest in the present war of SandWing succession.

*Though mostly a peaceful tribe, RainWings can actually be QUITE dangerous when we want to be! The SandWings were lucky our tribe had no interest in their stupid war. From our tranquilizer darts that can knock dragons out flat to our camouflage ability, RainWings are perfectly adapted to our rainforest home and know how to use its secrets to defend against intruders bent on wrongdoing. Oh, and P.S. did I mention our deadly venom? Only used in emergency situations, of course. — **Glory***

Few dragons have ventured into the rainforest and returned to tell the tale, and so our knowledge of the rainforest's plants and animals is quite limited. RainWings are the most isolated of any tribe — except for the mysterious, powerful NightWings, of course, whose kingdom's location is unknown.

CHALLENGES FOR THE RAINWING THRONE

AS TOLD BY HANDSOME TO QUEEN GLORY

Many, many years ago, our tribe was much less peaceful than we are today. We had to be, given that several other tribes coveted our beautiful rainforest. We had to defend ourselves against all kinds of attacks.

But some of those attacks came from within. Legend tells of a time when there were so many dragons vying for the RainWing throne that we went through eight queens in one moon cycle. Eight queens dead almost before they could enjoy a single suntime on the royal pavilion.

The same legend says it was the ninth queen who put an end to the bloodshed. She believed that each and every RainWing was vital to the tribe's survival. She said if we kept having our bravest, brightest, and strongest royal dragons murder each other in a mad scramble for power, our tribe would soon fall prey to one of the bigger and/or wealthier tribes.

And so she introduced the idea of royal challenges — contests for the throne that test our skills and strength, but don't end in death. Each queen had the right to choose the nature of the competition, or to invent her own if she wished. Now our peaceful transfer of power reflects the values of our peaceful tribe.

Here are some examples of royal challenges that we have seen in our tribe's recent history:

THE FRUIT-GATHERING TRIAL: The competing dragons are tasked to collect as many varieties of fruit as possible within a limited time.

THE TREETOP RACE: Dragons must fly three times outside the ring of trees of the Arboretum, touching down each circuit on the small platform high in the trees that marks the race's beginning and end.

THE STORYTELLING EVENT: Whichever dragon can tell the longest story with the fewest listeners falling asleep wins.

THE VENOM-TARGETING MATCH: Each dragon shoots her venom to see who can spit the farthest and which dragon can shoot more precisely. The dragon with the best overall score wins.

THE MEAL-PREPARATION CONTEST: Each dragon is given several ingredients that she must include in a special meal. The dragon who creates the tastiest meal wins.

THE FLOWER HUNT: A particular rare flower is hidden in the Arboretum and the first dragon to find it wins.

THE CAMOUFLAGE COMPETITION: Each dragon takes a turn camouflaging herself while the other dragon searches for her. The dragon who finds their competitor in the shortest amount of time wins.

THE SLOTH-TAMING TASK: Each dragon is introduced to a sloth she has never before encountered. The dragon who first successfully coaxes the sloth to climb onto her neck wins.

It is my hope that it will be many years before we see another challenge. But when that day comes, I am sure it will be as noble and fair as the long line of peaceful challenges preceding it.

EXPRESS YOUR FEELINGS IN FULL COLOR!

AS TOLD BY JAMBU OF THE RAINWINGS

I love being a RainWing. Don't you love it? I love being able to change my scales to any color I want! No other tribe can do that, and it's the coolest thing. We can choose to be something beautiful or something quiet or something that matches our friends' scales. Or we can use our scales to camouflage ourselves and disappear into the scenery around us.

(This one dragon queen I know thinks that this is "an excellent defensive battle strategy," but what it's *really* good for is hide-and-seek! RainWings are the *best* at hide-and-seek!)

But one really important thing to know about us is that our scales also change color with our emotions. Like, when I'm really happy, I turn pink all over! So yeah, true, I'm pretty much always pink. I mean, there's a lot to be happy about! Sloths, flying, papayas, my awesome sister, sunshine, not getting kidnapped by bad guys anymore, all that stuff. So excellent. Most pink-worthy!

Dragonets change color a *lot* because they have so many big emotions and they don't have much control over their scales yet. Adult dragons are better at controlling our scale colors if we have to — but we usually don't want to! RainWings believe that it's helpful for your friends to know how you're feeling . . . like, if you need help, or a

hug, or if you're just *so wildly happy* to see them! Sometimes it's hard to tell dragons how you feel with words, so it's great to show it with your scales instead.

Remember that most dragons won't be all one color at once. Emotions are complicated! Look for different colors appearing in patterns or in different places on the RainWing's body. That way you can figure out if they're sad but also a little bit mad, or sad and kind of sick, or extremely happy and sort of proud of something, or happy-surprised but also a little bit confused. (I'm a little bit confused sometimes!)

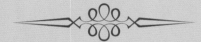

A GUIDE TO JAMBU'S FAVORITE RAINWING FEELING-COLORS:

GOLD SCALES: happy or excited

YELLOW SCALES: amused or surprised

LAVENDER SCALES: delighted

PINK-ROSE SCALES: joyful, happy (like me!), or in love (also like me!)

Unless a dragon is a really light pink — that might mean they're embarrassed! (And in love? I hear that sometimes those two go together!) — **Jambu**

BLUE SCALES: curious, calm, tranquil

Though if they turn cyan, *they're concentrating, and* light blue *scales can mean a dragon is sad, which always makes* me *sad!* — **Jambu**

JAMBU'S LEAST FAVORITE
RAINWING FEELING-COLORS:

RED SCALES: angry

ORANGE SCALES: irritated or frustrated

  THAT'S why Glory's wings are always orange! — **Tsunami**

  Only when I'm talking to you! — **Glory**

GREEN SCALES usually mean a dragon feels pretty bad, whether they're the *dark green* of distress or the *acid green* of shock/disbelief or the *pale green* of being scared

PURPLE SCALES: a range of emotions from guilty to proud — usually **DARK PURPLE** is a guiltier feeling, while a **LIGHTER VIOLET** color is closer to pride

ORANGEY-PURPLE SCALES: confused

WHITE SCALES: in pain or sick

BROWN SCALES: stressed out

  We don't see too many white or brown scales in the rainforest, unless someone is pretending to be an IceWing or a MudWing! — **Jambu**

DARK GRAY SCALES mean a dragon feels sorrowful, while a **BLUE-GRAY** dragon feels depressed, and a dragon with **BLACK SCALES** is deeply upset, possibly furious or hating something (we don't see that a lot either!).

I hope this guide helps everyone better understand your RainWing friends!

For many generations, the RainWings have lived without scrolls. They did not teach their dragonets to read or write; instead, they developed an oral storytelling tradition. They will often gather in groups before or after their suntime to share stories. Some of them are fragments of history or myth, passed down from long ago, but most RainWing storytellers focus on either the present moment or dreams of impossible, magical adventures.

I must admit I once thought their lives seemed rather dull and monotonous — but the more I learn about them, the more I see how vivid their imaginations are. There is more going on inside each of those brightly colored heads than anyone might guess, and I think it'll be fascinating to see what happens as they learn to write and begin to preserve some of those stories.

But RainWings were not always like this. From what we have been able to uncover so far, they were once more like the other kingdoms. In Darkstalker's time, they had scrolls and libraries; they traded and negotiated and occasionally fought with the other tribes. We are not sure about how or why they changed; so far, that seems to be a piece of history lost to time.

Much to our delight, however, two of our students found an ancient RainWing scroll buried in a library in Possibility. It appears to be a letter that was never sent, and it must be over a thousand years old. It is faded and torn — but what is in here is a fascinating glimpse at a very different RainWing tribe. This may be the oldest bit of RainWing writing in existence, and so we wanted to preserve it for this guide.

— Starflight

FOR QUEEN JACARANDA'S
EYES ONLY

WITH THANKS TO THE LIBRARY OF POSSIBILITY

Jacaranda,

You cannot carry on like this. You *must* not. I am your great-aunt and I have lived far longer than you, so I can see all your mistakes more clearly than you can. The changes you've made in your first year as queen are ridiculous! And appallingly shortsighted! I'm surprised my sister's ghost isn't haunting you with that ferociously disappointed expression of hers.

Don't you know that the RainWing tribe is supposed to be the terror of the continent? We are the dragons other dragons have nightmares about! We can be anywhere unseen. We can blend into the walls of palaces, the sands of the beaches, the trees of the forests. We can kill anyone almost instantly with just a few drops of venom in the right spot.

Dragons might fear the shadowy NightWings, who kill by moonlight, but during Queen Anaconda's rule, we were the dragons who killed by day, right in front of everyone! Invisible death, striking out of nowhere! Our most famous assassins have slain more powerful dragons than you can imagine!

So why, *why* would you shut down the assassin training program?

Why would you decree that our venom can never again be used on other dragons?

WHAT ARE YOU DOING TO ANACONDA'S ARMY?

I've heard reports that our fierce soldiers are now *weaving hammocks* and *teaching baby dragons to fly* and *making fruit salad*!

This is an outrage. They should be out fighting MudWings and clawing back territory from the SkyWings! Forget the stupid truce! Peace treaties are just delay tactics until you're strong enough to jump back in and start killing again! DID YOUR GRANDMOTHER TEACH YOU NOTHING?

Listen, I know the end of the last war was a mess. No one knew what the SkyWings had, or how much damage they could do. Yes, we lost a lot of rainforest and far too many dragons (although was it really half our tribe? Or is that just what you're telling everyone to scare them off from any more wars?). But no matter how bad it was, we could have fought on! My sister would *never* have surrendered, no matter how many RainWings died. She would have kept everyone fighting until she was the last RainWing left in Pyrrhia!

Perhaps I should have challenged her myself. If I'd taken the throne from Anaconda, perhaps one of my own daughters would have ended up on the throne instead of your spineless mother. She failed us so badly in the last war, I thought any queen would be better than her — and then you came along! The granddaughter of the great queen Anaconda, abiding by a peace treaty! I never thought I'd see the day. It's outrageous.

If you don't write back to me at once, I will be forced to leave the SandWing strong-hold to come investigate this horror show myself. It's not like I'm much use as a spy (or "ambassador," or whatever nonsense you're calling it now) if you're not interested in SandWing weaknesses and how to defeat them! I might as well come home and try to save our tribe from your ineptitude.

On swift wings,
Python

P.S. And WHAT is going on with the platforms and hammocks you're building at the top of the canopy? Did I hear correctly that these are for *napping*? Don't you know that too much sun will make our dragons as bad as sloths? (And yes, I know about your appalling obsession with taming prey, and I would like to know what we are supposed to eat if you insist on making all our food into pets!)

CHAPTER 4

NIGHTWINGS

QUEEN BATTLEWINNER
IN HER LAVA CAULDRON

North Beach

Queen
Vigilance's
Palace

NightWing
School

Great
Diamond

Library

VOLCANIC NIGHTWING KINGDOM

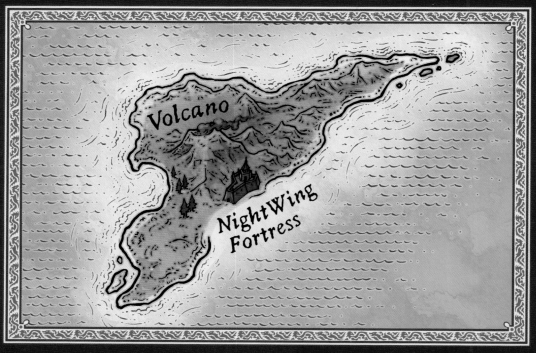

Volcano

NightWing
Fortress

NIGHTWINGS

SCALES: purplish-black

EYES: black or dark blue, dark green, or purple

UNUSUAL CHARACTERISTICS: scattered silver scales on the underside
of their wings, like a night sky full of stars; forked black tongues

ABILITIES: can breathe fire; disappear into dark shadows;
a limited few can read minds or foretell the future

HABITAT: previously a volcanic island north of the Pyrrhian continent; currently most of the tribe
live in the rainforest, with a few off trying to settle in the ruins of the ancient NightWing city

DIET: previously carrion; now their diet is adjusting to the available wildlife of the rainforest
(with a significant amount of pressure being applied by their vegetarian cohabitants!)

QUEEN: Queen Glory

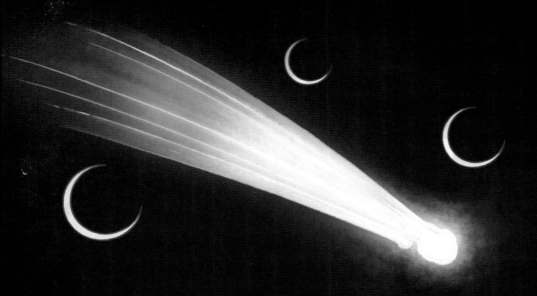

TALES OF THE NIGHTWINGS

Many moons ago, in the NightWing kingdom, there was a young dragonet who hatched without powers. Three silver crescents hung in the sky that night, but a blazing star as bright as a full moon lit the darkness. And so the dragonet's parents named him Comet, believing he was as shining and special as that shooting star, and surely destined for greatness.

Before long, though, it became clear that Comet could neither see the future nor sense the thoughts of those around him. When he was old enough to go to school, his classmates teased him for his lack of powers. "What makes you so special?" they taunted. "How could a powerless dragon ever do anything great or important?" Those with mind-reading powers mocked his resentful, worried thoughts. Those with the power of prophecy laughed at all the boring uselessness ahead of him.

Only one dragon, Mindhealer, was kind to Comet. Mindhealer was a skilled reader of other dragons' emotions and always comforted Comet when the others were cruel.

Years went by as Comet worked hard at his lessons, reading every scroll he could find and flying all over the NightWing kingdom until he could map every inch of it. He knew each rock and stream and coastline, each cave and every mountaintop. Even without powers, he hoped to do something with his hard work to bring honor to his tribe.

One beautiful clear day in high summer, Comet was out flying when he suddenly found himself in a terrible storm that had appeared from nowhere. Wind and rain blew every which way, roaring like a thousand angry dragons. Comet clawed his way in the direction he thought was up until he found himself above the storm, staring at an impossible starry sky with two full moons. And then, just as suddenly, he was back in the blue sunlit sky, without a cloud — or a moon — to be seen.

Comet flew back as fast as he could to find Mindhealer. He told him what had happened, and Mindhealer said, "Comet, you've had a vision."

And thus Comet realized that, at long last, his powers had been revealed. He was a seer, after all.

Together, Comet and Mindhealer flew to the palace to warn the queen. She listened and then she laughed, for her own dragonets were Comet's classmates and had told her of the silly dragonet with no powers. Mindhealer and Comet tried in vain to convince the queen, but for days she would not listen, even when her own seers started having visions of doom and destruction, of a mighty hurricane that would sweep away her kingdom.

But not one of her seers knew when the storm would come, or how to save the kingdom. Only Comet had seen the two full moons, and he knew how soon the danger would strike. Comet and Mindhealer found every dragon who believed Comet and every dragon who loved a dragon who believed Comet. Soon they had gathered the whole kingdom and flew with them to the highest mountain peaks Comet knew, where there were caves to keep them safe. And there the NightWings waited as a great hurricane blew through their kingdom.

Although the storm brought terrible destruction, all the NightWings were saved. And ever afterward, on those rare occasions when Comet had a vision, no matter how small, his tribe always listened.

This was Starflight's favorite scroll when he lived under the mountain. I have no idea why! It's so quiet and I don't like the sad parts where Comet is sad. I guess Starflight didn't have any scrolls about The Prophetess, who was the most awesome super dragon ever and flew around bam-bam-bamming bad guys with her visions all day long. SHE was the BEST and there were NO SAD BITS about dragons being mean to her (because if they ever tried she would tell them all the terrible things in their future, ha ha!). (And sometimes she would BE the terrible things in their future! So fierce!) — **Fatespeaker**

Fatespeaker, this Comet legend is a story of faith and perseverance and heroism. Those Prophetess stories are ridiculous. — **Starflight**

ORRRR are they prophetic tales of a dragon with visions who will ONE DAY be the MOST AWESOME SEER WHO EVER LIVED. — **Fatespeaker**

Pretty sure they're just ridiculous. — **Starflight**

I guess WE SHALL SEE. — **Fatespeaker**

Dear Starflight,

I think there have been enough scrolls written in the last few centuries about how great and wonderful NightWings are, don't you? Our tribe managed to distribute stories like that far and wide across Pyrrhia, although most of them are a little unreliable, to say the least. Wildly overexaggerated, one might even say. (I had to sit on Qibli to stop him from adding what *he* would call them!) Even if we needed a new one, though, I'm afraid I would be the wrong dragon to write it, as I did not grow up with my tribe.

So instead I hope it's all right that I've written up a report on what I've learned about NightWing powers. I like the idea of your guide bringing the truth to all the tribes at last. Most of this I learned from Darkstalker, but I double-checked all these facts in the scrolls from the library in the old Night Kingdom.

THE TRUTH ABOUT NIGHTWING POWERS
BY MOONWATCHER OF THE NIGHTWINGS

Not all NightWings have powers.

In order for a NightWing dragonet to develop either of the potential NightWing powers, their egg must be hatched under at least one full moon. Eggs like this will turn from black to silver soon before they hatch.

The three moons are named Oracle, Perception, and Imperial (the largest).

Dragons that hatch under one full moon are gifted with either the power of mind reading or of prophecy, while dragons that hatch under two full moons have both powers.

It's very rare for a dragon to be born under three full moons, like Darkstalker was. He said that being born under the third moon made the powers of mind reading and prophecy stronger. (Some believe there is a lunar connection with animus magic, but Darkstalker was quite sure that animus power was passed down genetically, although sometimes it might hide within families for generations before appearing again.)

Dragons with mind-reading powers normally have silver scales shaped like teardrops near the outer corners of their eyes, although it seems this is not a guarantee they will have that power.

In the ancient Night Kingdom, careful planning went into making sure that as many eggs as possible hatched under full moons, and empowered dragons were common. Once the tribe fled to the volcanic island, however, they lived under a sky clogged with smoke and hatched their eggs in underground caverns, and the vaunted NightWing abilities became more legend than reality.

However, now that NightWings are living in the rainforest and the old Night Kingdom, under the moonlit sky once again, it seems likely that we'll start to see more NightWings with powers in the years ahead.

Suggestion: Starflight, maybe one day we can start a class for seers and mind readers? To help them learn about their new powers and how to use them for good? So they won't be totally overwhelmed and freaked out by them? Just an idea.

See you soon,
Moonwatcher

STUDYING THE STUDIERS:
INTERVIEW WITH A NIGHTWING

The following interview was conducted on a cloudy, drizzly day in the rainforest, but let it be noted that the grayness of the sky above did nothing to dim the brilliant, dazzling inner and outer light of the interviewer, one Queen Glory of the RainWings and NightWings.

GLORY: Deathbringer, just write down what we say. Don't you dare add any extra Deathbringer nonsense. [she said in the most regal and majestic way]

DEATHBRINGER: I have no idea what "Deathbringer nonsense" would even look like. I am an extremely serious dragon. I will only write serious things, like "The queen had brought along her favorite dragon in the world to transcribe the interview, because she trusted him in every way and knew she couldn't possibly live without him. Sometimes literally, as in the case of several NightWing assassination attempts."

GLORY: THAT nonsense. Don't put that in there! What are you writing now? This is for a book that other dragons will actually read, you marmoset.

DEATHBRINGER: Oh, I'm sure Starflight will edit out anything irrelevant.

[Starflight, Queen Glory specifically orders you to keep every word I am writing! Except maybe *marmoset*. Let's change that to you *incorrigible handsome rogue*. Ooo, yes, that's definitely what she actually said.]

At this point, the two dragons arrived at the quicksand prison of a certain NightWing prisoner by the name of Mastermind.

HER MOST GLORIOUS MAJESTY, QUEEN GLORY: Hello there.

THE SNIVELING CRIMINAL, MASTERMIND: Your Majesty. It is an honor to see you.

THE STALWART BODYGUARD, DEATHBRINGER: Hello, could you please muster up some cowering and cringing, or at least an awestruck expression? You look suspiciously serene in there.

MASTERMIND: I have learned that the less I move, the slower I sink. In point of fact, I am quite likely the world's leading expert on quicksand by now. All I have to do all day long is focus on breathing and being still. It has been surprisingly peaceful, after years of frantically trying to solve every NightWing problem before the entire tribe perished beneath the molten lava.

DEATHBRINGER: Is that why you chose this prison instead of the other?

MASTERMIND (visibly shuddering): You mean that oppressive death box Darkstalker made? That dreadful place was far too much like the volcanic island: sunless, lifeless, soul-sucking.

GLORY: I hate it, too. We're going to let vines grow over it and pretend it isn't there.

MASTERMIND: I am prostrate with gratitude that Your Majesty allowed me to return here instead. Even a lifetime of imprisonment will be bearable so long as I can experience the warmth of the sun and the wind on my face.

GLORY: Well, hang on, nobody said anything about lifetime imprisonment, Lord Dramatic. You know your trial starts next week. It just took a while to find a balance between the RainWings who wanted to punish you and the ones who were ready to forgive you immediately, which honestly was most of them because they're too kind for their own good.

MASTERMIND: Kindness was in such short supply on our island. My guards here have all been astonishingly kind. I cannot help but wonder if this is an inborn trait, somehow environmental, or perhaps cultural — aren't you curious how they came to be like this? You'd be a fascinating subject for this study, growing up as you did, removed from the environment and the culture. My hypothesis from considering your situation is that the trait is not innate, although to be sure we'd have to find other RainWings raised apart from the rest of the tribe —

DEATHBRINGER: Excuse me. If you are trying to suggest that Queen Glory is *not* kind, I would like to draw your attention to the fact that *you* are for some reason still alive, and so are all the rest of the NightWings. *My* hypothesis is that she could easily have fed you to piranhas and no one would have minded.

MASTERMIND: That is — yes, quite right, that is true, I apologize. My brain spins off along these tangents, and I say all the wrong things, don't I? But yes, the kindness: three walks a day and all the food I can eat; it is more than any NightWing deserves, especially me. I feel I have learned more from my guards here than from all my years with Queen Battlewinner. I regret . . . I truly regret how unkind we were to our captives, Your Majesty.

GLORY: "Unkind" is one way to put it. I'm afraid I'm not as naturally forgiving as most of my tribe. But we'll find a way for you to atone for what you did.

MASTERMIND: Perhaps some inventions to improve their lives? I have so many ideas!

GLORY: Perhaps. I like the idea of bringing science and learning to my RainWings, but you must promise to both teach them and *listen* to them.

MASTERMIND: I will. I promise I will.

GLORY: Well, we'll see how the trial goes. Starflight says hello, by the way. Did yesterday's guard read you his last letter?

MASTERMIND: Yes, Your Majesty. If I may say so, he is an extraordinary writer and works so hard on his library. I am so proud of him.

GLORY: Yeah, he's all right. So you understand this interview? For his book?

MASTERMIND: I believe so.

GLORY: He sent, like, a GIANT list of questions, but I have two tribes to govern, so if he really wants all these answers, he'll have to come visit you himself. I'll just do a couple. So here's one: Why are NightWings so insufferably smug about themselves?

MASTERMIND: Three moons. Did he actually write that?

GLORY: I might be paraphrasing.

MASTERMIND: Well, I — I suppose that's how we were raised. We've always been taught to believe that NightWings are a superior tribe at some inherent, genetic level. No other tribe has powers like ours, after all —

GLORY: Sure, but other tribes have animus dragons, or firescales like Peril, or blood-red eggs like the MudWing tribe —

DEATHBRINGER: Or magical death spit!

GLORY (giving Deathbringer a thoroughly marvelous glare that is impossible to capture in words): And you don't see any of them lording it over the rest.

MASTERMIND: Truly? Doesn't every dragon think their own tribe is the best?

DEATHBRINGER: Not me.

GLORY: Maybe some of them, but only one tribe had a decades-long sinister prophecy plan to manipulate everyone.

MASTERMIND: That plan was hatched out of desperation. We believed in our greatness, but we had had no evidence of it for so long. We were starving and soon to be homeless, if any of us survived the next eruption at all. Everything we wrote in the scrolls, every lie we told, was to save ourselves.

GLORY: You should have just asked for help. The RainWings would have helped you.

MASTERMIND: We did not know that. We had no scrolls about RainWings in our library. We knew so little about them after hiding ourselves away for centuries that even their venom came as a surprise to us, and we thought they must be dangerous if they had such a weapon. Besides, we could not let our weakness show, especially after trumpeting our strength for so long. We thought we had to take what we needed by force, but all we had, to begin with, was Morrowseer's prophecy. All we had were the stories other dragons believed about us.

GLORY: Fine. Deathbringer, write down "smugness based on lies and insecurity." I guess they're not the only dragons I've met with that particular tendency. Next question: Is there anything actually good about NightWings?

MASTERMIND: I believe so . . . I hope so. Our love of learning, our respect for science, our libraries and laboratories and schools that were once the envy of Pyrrhia, before we had to flee our original kingdom. Did you know we were the first tribe to develop a written Dragon language? We taught it to all the other tribes so everyone could record our history and communicate with one another. According to our most ancient scrolls, there used to be traveling NightWing teachers who crisscrossed the continent, bringing scrolls and stories to every tribe.

GLORY: Really? How do I know these aren't more NightWing lies to make your tribe seem awesome?

MASTERMIND: There are records in the scrolls of other tribes. If anything survived the volcano, I can show you our library, where SandWing and SeaWing and IceWing scrolls will confirm all this. There are also architectural plans and correspondence records from NightWing scriptoriums, where dragons copied out scrolls by talon, over and over, so every dragon in Pyrrhia could have scrolls of their own if they wanted.

GLORY: Three moons, Starflight will love that. Deathbringer, write: "Yes, Starflight, simmer down, we can have a meeting about starting our own scriptorium and traveling teacher program."

MASTERMIND: We were also the tribe who first took medicine seriously; our ancestors discovered and recorded most of the healing treatments used by all the tribes today. And once upon a time, our seers used their visions to protect dragons from harm, no matter which tribe they were from. Back then we were better at sharing our knowledge — but we can be like that again! With better leadership and a safe home and a future for our dragonets, NightWings can become the tribe we once were: bringing knowledge and healing to the world.

GLORY: Hmmm. I wouldn't mind seeing that. All right, it's time for your walk, and I think that's enough for Starflight, don't you, Deathbringer?

DEATHBRINGER: Let me just add one more thing about the luminous queen's gifted mind clearly developing plans before our very eyes —

GLORY: Yes, plans to fill your hammock with rhinoceros beetles if you keep calling me silly things like "luminous." By all the moons, you ~~squashy papaya~~ incredibly dashing hero.

STARFLIGHT!
STOP SENDING ME ANNOYING NOTES!
I AM BUSY!

SO WHAT IF YOU ARE MY BROTHER?
WHAT GOOD HAS THAT EVER DONE ME? NONE,
STARFLIGHT! ZERO PILES OF GOOD!

TALONS AND TAILS, I DON'T CARE
ABOUT YOUR STUPID BOOK!

AAAAAAAAAAAAAAAAAAAAAARGH, FINE,
if it will stop your delusional girlfriend from showing
up on my doorstep every other day, I will write you
ONE THING for your sappy little project.

RISING FROM THE RUINS

BY FIERCETEETH OF THE NIGHTWINGS

Yes, we have set up a sort of encampment in the ruins of the ancient NightWing kingdom.

There are about twenty-seven of us living here.

I am basically in charge. I can't get anyone to call me Queen Fierceteeth, but I am clearly the bossiest and the smartest, so it's only a matter of time.

We're not quite big enough to call ourselves the Night Kingdom again. But we think we could be the size of Sanctuary or even Possibility someday, so we're going to call our settlement something like Knowledge or Freedom or Resurrection or Atonement. New Beginnings, maybe. Or Renewal. Something properly fancy-sounding.

Every month, Glory has been sending us food and seeds and wood and medicinal herbs and all kinds of things, entirely without anyone asking her to. At first I was furious about that, because who does she think she is? She's not our queen! That's the whole point of why we stayed here, those of us who decided not to go back to the rainforest!

But then she offered to trade for scrolls from the library and asked if she could send teams to study the old city, so, now that it's a trade situation, I have grumpily decided that it's all right.

This is a harder place to live than the rainforest, that's for sure. Only tough, strong dragons will make it here. We can't just pluck prey from the branches and lounge around eating all day long. The wind off the sea and the mountains is bracingly cold, and the structures of the old city are dangerously unstable. (Judging by the oldest maps, about half the peninsula crumbled into the sea sometime in the last two thousand years.)

But we can <u>breathe</u>.

We can hunt and we can fly and we can see the moons every night.

(Here's something your weird sciencey brain might geek out about: all of us have stopped sleeping through the night. We are mostly nocturnal now, rising late in the day to get the last afternoon sunlight, then hunting throughout the night, under the moons, and returning to sleep shortly after sunrise. Maybe that's how our ancestors did it? Or maybe it just worked out best for us that way. The moons seem very bright here, and there is so much prey out after dark. Prey that we can easily sneak up on, with our dark scales. I ate an entire WOLF two nights ago, Starflight! It did not taste like chicken; I don't know where you got that idea. Unless maybe an angry, furry chicken that spent its whole life running around hitting other chickens with an ax and then setting them on fire.)

I am not a sentimental sappy scrollworm like you, and I don't give two smoldering coyotes about ancient history at all. But I guess it is kind of cool to fly around the old city and see how big and elaborate it was.

Like, we found something that must have been a _theatre_. There was a stage and rows of seats and a whole backstage area scattered with faded scripts and rusty props. It looked exactly the way I pictured from old scrolls like _A Midsummer NightWing's Dream_ and _The Importance of Being a NightWing_ and _A Little NightWing Music_.

You wouldn't know this, but we were never allowed any time for theatre or art or music on the NightWing island. While you were probably painting your feelings and singing about your great life on the mainland, we were stuck in lessons on survival, science, and superiority.

But once upon a time, there was a whole civilization here. A healthy tribe who cared about art and beautiful architecture and gardens with NONEDIBLE PLANTS IN THEM. Bonecruncher has been digging around in the overgrown plots and in the gardening section of the library, and he says they planted completely purposeless things all the time just because they were pretty. We're not going to go quite that mad; we need all the food we can get right now.

(Bonecruncher also wants to change his name to Greentalon, which is all I need. Our names are great NightWing names! Greentalon sounds suspiciously RainWingish to me! I hope he doesn't start a stupid trend. I'd better not end up living with a bunch of Cuddleheads and Snugglebutts!)

Anyway, so a few of the dragons are thinking about trying to put on a real play. I suppose I'll send you an invite if we pull it together.

ARRRGH, how did this get so long! You are so irritating, Starflight! Look at all this time you made me waste! Do NOT bother me again for at least a year; I don't want to hear from you!

— Fierceteeth

P.S. But in about a year, I guess I'll have to see your boring face again if you want to come for the hatching ceremony. Not that you have to! I couldn't care less! Stay in your library sniffing scrolls forever for all I care! But I guess apparently family is usually invited to these things and you're all I've got. And even though you're a useless brother, I guess maybe you might be an all right uncle, perhaps. Which is to say, yes, Strongwings and I are having eggs soon; at least three, I think, from the stupid annoying size of me. Three! In one hatching! Just another sign that we should have left that moonsforsaken island YEARS earlier. Anyway, they'll be the first eggs to hatch here, hopefully under a full moon or two, so if you're interested in meeting your nieces (and maybe a nephew, I suppose), I guess you can come do that.

P.P.S. But do NOT make a big deal out of this! I have heard about the parties SkyWings throw for their hatching ceremonies and they sound completely ridiculous.

P.P.P.S. You may, however, send as many gifts as you like, starting now.

ON QUEEN VIGILANCE'S GLASS JUBILEE

WITH THANKS TO THE LIBRARY OF RENEWAL

beloved queen is the guardian not only of our tribe but also of our heritage. Under her stewardship, the tribe has revived certain ancient customs such as the full moon music festival, as well as continued longstanding traditions such as our ceremony for seers and mind readers. With her deep appreciation of our history, Queen Vigilance has also begun new traditions, including the Glass Jubilee, which will soon be held to mark the forty years of her reign.

The full moon music festival offers our gifted musicians an opportunity to share their newest compositions while also introducing our young dragonets to traditional NightWing music. Recently Queen Vigilance decreed that each festival should include an hour when amateur performers may also share their talents. Her royal offspring have been kind enough to grace us with their own performances from time to time.

The annual ceremony honoring those of our tribe who have come into their powers stretches back hundreds, if not thousands, of years. This event celebrates the gifts of our noble tribe and Queen Vigilance presides over the solemn, yet joyful, ritual. Each seer offers a vision of our glorious future, and our mind readers share the outpouring of adoration for Queen Vigilance and our tribe that they can hear in the minds and hearts of all NightWings.

Queen Vigilance is also a keen scholar of our tribe's history. Her support was instrumental to the creation of the island temple honoring the first librarians of our tribes. This temple recognizes the many contributions our early librarians made to securing the vast knowledge of the NightWings. Without their diligent — and at times dangerous! — work, many scrolls from centuries past would be lost to the dust of time or would never have been written in the first place.

Queen Vigilance's Glass Jubilee will be a testament not only to the splendor of her reign, but also the longstanding intellectual and artistic superiority of the NightWings. From intricate, elegant glasswork created by our artisans to wonderful games, beautiful music, and graceful dancing by attendees, the festival will be an enormous success that all future queens' festivals will emulate.

As Queen Vigilance's reign stretches into its fifth decade, she will

CHAPTER 5
SANDWINGS

QUEEN THORN
WITH SMOLDER AND FLOWER

SANDWINGS

SCALES: pale gold or white scales the color of desert sand

EYES: black

UNUSUAL CHARACTERISTICS: poisonous barbed tail; forked black tongues

ABILITIES: can survive a long time without water; poison enemies with the tip of their tail like scorpions; bury themselves for camouflage in the desert sand; breathe fire

HABITAT: the vast scorched desert west of the mountains

DIET: lizards, cactus, desert rodents, occasionally camels, but they prefer to eat light

QUEEN: Queen Thorn

 IN SEARCH OF
THE LOST TREASURES OF THE SANDWING QUEEN

When Queen Oasis died, some of her treasure was stolen by scavengers, but most was taken by Blister. The items stolen by the scavengers have been found, but Blister's haul is still missing.

HAVE YOU SEEN THIS TREASURE? HAVE YOU HEARD A RUMOR OF WHERE IT MIGHT BE? ARE YOU ONE OF BLISTER'S FORMER SOLDIERS?

IF YOU KNOW ANYTHING, SEND A MESSAGE TO SMOLDER AT THE SANDWING PALACE.
YOU MIGHT EVEN GET A REWARD!

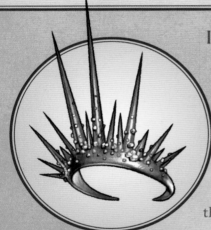

THE DESERT TIARA – This tiara, worn by SandWing queens for centuries, is wrought from silver into spikes resembling cactus spines and sprinkled with crystals to represent the precious oasis water of the SandWing Kingdom.

THE TWILIGHT NECKLACE – This necklace is a long, thin coiled chain made of a silvery-black metal. Possibly of NightWing origin. Care should also be taken with this item.

THE SANDWING SCEPTER – The scepter is a staff of oak wood, plated with beaten gold and inlaid with onyx and pearls. Records suggest the scepter is purely ornamental and not animus-touched, but care should be used handling the scepter, just in case.

ASSORTED GEMS AND COINS – Likely in bags stamped with Queen Oasis's symbol.

Hi Starflight!

Have I mentioned lately how excited I am about your guide? You always wanted to write a scroll and now you're doing it! And it's so official *and* researchy *and it's going to make the world a better place, and I love it love it love it. I can't wait to read all the stories from the tribes who never get to write their own scrolls.*

Thank you for asking me to help with cataloging the weirdling collection and whether I'd be all right going back into it. It was pretty traumatic being stuck in there when I was a prisoner, but it wasn't for long, and I had Flower with me. And I never think about it anymore now that Burn is gone. Mostly never.

Burn's collection was creepy because she hurt dragons and other creatures to build it (and also partly because she kept it all in a creepy tower with eerie lighting!). There were all kinds of strange things in there, and some of them were funny-looking dragons who had their own lives and families she stole them from. I wish we could learn more about them so we could understand them as real dragons, not weird specimens.

Anyway, Smolder and I went through what he kept before Thorn destroyed the tower. I'm sending along a list of some of the more interesting (and less gruesome — mostly!) items. Some of them I remember from my stay in the tower, but others I'd never seen before.

Thorn said we could bring some of this back to the academy if you'd like. (I think not the parts of dragons — I don't want to upset any of our students. Or, honestly, me!) Smolder also offered to send you the letters Burn stole that he's been trying to go through. He says he thinks you would learn a lot about the tribes from them. I think he's just getting tired of trying to figure out how to get them to the dragons they were meant for however long ago. You don't have to say yes! But I thought you'd probably want to see at least some of them.

I hope you find this information helpful! Tell everyone I miss them and I'll see you soon!

Love,
Sunny

FROM BURN'S COLLECTION

WHITE DRAGON: I saw this white dragon, with little wing stubs but no wings, when I was in the tower. The dragon who brought it to Burn said it was the offspring of a SandWing and an IceWing and so it was stunted because it was a hybrid, but I'm not sure I believe that and neither does Smolder. (We've met a lot of hybrids now, and they're all perfectly healthy and fine!) It's possible these stubs are actually wingbuds, like you told me SilkWings have before they go through their Metamorphosis. But this dragon only has two wingbuds, not four, and I don't think SilkWings are usually white. Could it be a tribe we haven't met yet? Or a dragon that came out different because of something that happened to its egg? Poor dragon.

DRAGONBITE VIPER SKIN: Smolder gasped when he saw this snakeskin because it looked so much like the snake that killed Burn. She'd gotten it years ago and used it to scare Blister once, which could be what gave Blister the idea to use vipers to kill Burn.

BURN'S FISH TANK: *Of course* Smolder saved Burn's tank full of glowing sea creatures — he is very good with pets! Inside are fish with strange bulging eyes and many flippers, seahorses with sharp teeth, very gloopy snails, and something that looks like an octopus but with way too many arms. Let's see if Turtle or Anemone can identify any of them for us!

BLOOD-RED MUDWING EGG WITH A CRACKED SHELL: Burn's soldiers said that around the time of the brightest night, she made them spy on MudWing nests and try to steal a blood-red egg. They found this one and brought it to her, but it never hatched, so she threw it against the wall (and almost hit Smolder).

HALF A WING, SPECKLED PURPLE AND GRAY: I remember this wing from my time in the tower. Smolder says it washed up on the beach in the SandWing kingdom. It must be Pantalan, and I'm pretty sure it looks like it's from a SilkWing — but, oh, how terrible to think of a SilkWing flying almost to Pyrrhia and then drowning! How could one have flown so far all alone?

STUFFED NIGHTWING (partially destroyed): Burn's soldiers told me this dragon boasted about an animus-touched object — a shiny blue sapphire, in fact — and refused to give it to Burn, so she killed him and mounted his corpse in her collection. The sapphire was never found, but while Scarlet was imprisoned here, she tore apart everything she could reach in a fit of rage, including this dragon. I think he must have swallowed the sapphire before Burn killed him, and that must be how and where Scarlet found the dreamvisitor — *inside* the NightWing.

JERBOA WITH HER DAUGHTER JERBOA II

Hey Starflight,

Sunny and Thorn said you were curious about my early days of taking care of Flower. I did actually keep a journal for a while back then, so I'm sending you what I wrote during the first week she was in the stronghold. It is wildly embarrassing to reread now, especially knowing what we now know about scavengers — but also because I had so many emotions and apparently no restraint in pouring them out everywhere.

Twenty years with Burn stomped that right out of me. Thorn says it would be marvelous if I would express an authentic emotion now and then, which I think is not entirely fair. "Wryly concerned" is an emotion, is it not? "Overcome with admiration but also brimming with helpful suggestions" — that should count, too, don't you think? Or there's always "quietly content and surprised and relieved to be alive." I express that one all the time, I think. She just needs to notice a little more carefully.

I hope this is what you were looking for. In retrospect, I really do believe that getting Flower is the best thing that ever happened to me.

Wishing you bright sun and strong winds,
Smolder

STRANGE TIME FOR
A NEW PET

What am I doing?

There's a small thing in my room and now it's mine forever and what was I thinking?

I'm in no shape to take care of a new pet.

The whole stronghold is in an uproar, and my life has fallen apart, and yet for some mysterious reason I've decided now is the perfect time to adopt a weird little creature that nobody knows anything about. (Oh, and P.S. maybe it murdered our mom? So it might also be super dangerous?)

Right. Very clever, Smolder. Top-notch brain working so well there.

My brother Singe says I should take notes on my new pet so I can learn how to take care of it. No one here has any idea how to raise a scavenger. No one's had a pet scavenger in the SandWing stronghold in years and years, maybe even centuries. Not many dragons have had a pet at all, because Mother or Burn or Blister would probably eat them or "accidentally" step on them.

STABBY

SPECIES: Scavenger

SIZE: Small, I think

PERSONALITY: Very squeaky, very
fierce. Good thing its teeth and claws
are so blunt and useless.

It keeps *watching* me. Like, it stares at me all the time with this intense little curious face.

Oh, it probably thinks I'm going to eat it. Well, Stabby, I'm not. That's not the plan anyway. The plan is you're my pet now, but, honestly, I can't guarantee another dragon won't wander through, think you're a snack, and eat you. That seems pretty likely.

Three moons, how am *I* supposed to keep this tiny animal alive? I feel like I can barely breathe. I haven't slept in days. I haven't been able to think straight since Palm disappeared. I don't know if she's alive or dead or if Mother got her or what happened to her and it's all I can think about. I can't possibly be responsible for a small, fluffy, loud creature who keeps trying to escape even though it's injured. No matter how cute it is.

My other brother Scald says that's exactly why I should keep it, though. He says I need distracting.

But maybe now that Mother is dead, Palm will come back . . .

Singe and Scald think there's no way Palm is still alive.

If we had waited just *a few more days* before trying to elope, she'd still be here and Mother would be dead and we could be together.

I can't think about that.

I can't throw myself in the nearest fire either, because then someone will definitely eat my poor scavenger.

Poor little Stabby. Little fierce-face trying to pick fights with dragons, waving a tiny sword around. So, there's an observation: they're not very smart! But they are pretty cute, or at least, Stabby is.

My new pet seems to be having some trouble walking. I mean, it's weird that they walk on two legs instead of four at all, but even one of those legs seems to not be working right. I'm guessing that's why Stabby didn't run away with the other scavengers who stole the treasure. Which puts my scavenger in a much better situation than those scavengers, because Burn and most of the army have gone chasing after them, and that means fire and crunching and very bad ends for anything they catch.

I guess I could try to describe my new pet. Stabby has long flowy dark fur on the top of its head and clever little paws and gigantic brown eyes, like a baby fennec fox. Sometimes it looks as sad as I feel, which I know is silly because it's just an animal, but I kind of like having something else in the room to mope with.

You know, I'm realizing I really don't want anyone to eat my scavenger.

I've put it in a birdcage Six-Claws brought me from the kitchen, which I think we usually keep small birds in before cooking them. The scavenger was very unhappy about this and did its best to squeeze through the bars, but with no success. Finally it must have worn itself out, because it's asleep now.

It sleeps curled up in a little ball on its side with its tiny paws under its head.

It's so small.

I probably should be writing about my feelings about Mother being mysteriously murdered and the royal succession crisis we're suddenly in. But honestly, Mother was awful and I won't miss her at all, and I don't care which of my sisters gets the throne.

I don't care about anything now that Palm is gone.

All right, maybe I care a tiny tiny bit about keeping this scavenger alive.

I guess I have to get up in the morning and keep going for a bit longer so I can figure out what to feed it. Poor thing didn't want anything to do with the dead mouse I dropped into the cage for it.

Well. Tomorrow is another day.

Good night, Stabby.

This morning when I woke up, Stabby had somehow climbed to the top of its cage and was trying to squeeze through the bars up there. Maybe partly to get away from the dead mouse, which did not smell great.

I threw the mouse away and took Stabby and the whole cage with me to see Six-Claws, who is probably the most sensible dragon I know, and usually very good at solving problems. Today, however, he was wildly uninterested in helping me figure out what to feed a scavenger.

"Prince Smolder," he said, looking concerned, or maybe exasperated. "I was up all night burning a scavenger den and then searching the ashes with no luck. The queen is dead and everything in the royal treasury is missing. No one knows who is going to rule the SandWings now. Everything is rather a mess. I don't have time to help with strange new pets."

And then Burn came storming into the barracks, followed by Blister and my brothers.

"*There* you are!" she yelled at me. "Give me that scavenger! I'm going to cut off its head and mount it on a spike for everyone to see!"

"No!" I threw myself between her and the cage. "You can't kill it! It's mine!"

"I most certainly can!" she roared. "That thing killed our mother! We need vengeance! We need to show other tribes that nobody gets away with assassinating SandWing royalty!"

"Oh yesss," Blister hissed. "That will be very intimidating. Here's the tiny head of the tiny mammal who managed to take down the SandWing queen, on display to remind everyone of how very, very tiny it was."

Burn snarled at her.

"Oh, just let Smolder keep it," Singe said dismissively. "You know how Mother has been treating him lately. He can have *one* nice thing, come on."

"Yeah," Scald said. "Nobody cares about this little creature. They only want to know about the treasure and the throne. I say let Smolder have it."

"Besides, look, he loves it so much already," Singe added, cackling. "Have you picked out a name for it, little brother? Squishy-Squashy Flufferkins?"

"Its NAME is STABBY," I said, with great dignity, I thought, but that sent both of my brothers off into peals of laughter.

There was a bit more arguing after that, but they finally convinced Burn I could keep it, and then they told me to go away so they could discuss the throne, so I went to the library to see if there were any scrolls about scavengers there.

Of course there weren't, but there was a scroll for dragonets on pets in general, so I took that one, even though it seemed kind of weird.

Like, the first chapter is *How to Choose Your Pet! — armadillo? coyote? or maybe a nice snake would be the right speed for you, just make sure it's not a dragonbite viper, ha ha!* Then it includes recipes for if you get bored and decide to eat your pet instead, which I thought was rather gruesome for a dragonets' scroll.

The next chapter is about feeding pets, and it has charts of carnivores and herbivores so you can figure out what yours is, but scavengers weren't on there.

"Are you a plant-eater?" I asked Stabby. "Is that why you didn't want the mouse?"

Stabby was lying on the bottom of the empty birdcage looking very tired and droopy, which made me quite worried. I rolled ahead in the scroll and the word *water* jumped out at me. Oh no! Mammals need a lot more water than us, don't they? Most animals need more water than SandWing dragons do.

I picked up the cage and ran to the kitchen. Ostrich was in there — she's Six-Claws's mother and one of the nicer kitchen workers. She brought me a small bowl of water with only a slightly puzzled look on her face, and I opened the cage door to put it inside.

Quick as a wink, Stabby leaped to its feet and bolted (limping) for the opening. I barely slammed the door shut again in time. It grabbed the bars and shook them and then shook its tiny paws at me and squeaked for a while.

"It was tricking me!" I said, delighted. "Did you see that? It's so clever!"

Ostrich did not look as impressed as I was, but she kept watching as Stabby finally stopped hollering and went over to the water. The scavenger stuck its whole head into the water, then scooped some into its mouth with its little clever paws, then climbed right into the bowl and used the rest to rinse off the sand it was covered in. You have literally never seen anything cuter.

I set the cage on a windowsill when it was done with the water so the sun could dry off the scavenger and its wrappings, and then I asked Ostrich for some fruit or cactus or something that an herbivore might eat.

She looked skeptical, but she gave me a handful of dates, which I slid through the bars of the cage. Stabby inspected them for a while, then took them over to sit in a patch of sun and nibble on them.

That's right! It liked the dates! I felt like an absolute genius. I'd figured out what scavengers like to eat on my second guess! I couldn't wait to share this with Palm — and then I remembered, and then I realized that I'd managed to forget about losing Palm for a whole five minutes.

We spent the rest of the day in my room. I read some more of the pet scroll, but mostly I stared out the window and sighed a lot, and I'm pretty sure that's what Stabby was doing, too.

Anyway, that's what I learned today. Scavengers are herbivores, and they especially like dates, and I have to remember to give it water every day.

Good night, Stabby.

Today our librarian told me that my scavenger is a girl, and when I asked him how he knew that, he said everyone knows that all female scavengers have longer head fur and are better climbers than male scavengers. I am not sure either of those is true, but I'm going to call Stabby "she" from now on, because I think other dragons are more likely to eat an "it" than a "she." (That might be optimistic of me — I had to chase off two different hungry dragonets this afternoon!)

I gave Stabby dates again this morning and she ate them happily, but when I brought her more dates in the evening, she looked at them, then looked at me and yibber-squeaked for about a decade. When I was like, "what? what's wrong with your favorite food?" she pointed through the bars at the meal that had been set out for me in my room.

"That's *my* food," I said patiently. "For *dragons*. This scroll clearly says *do not feed your pets dragon food, or they will get spoiled and want it all the time*. It *also* says I should *definitely* not feed you from the table."

Stabby stamped her feet and yabber-yelled and it was very adorable and OK, fine, I ended up giving her a little bit of everything I was eating. And guess what? She ate ALL of it, except the scrap of camel. Isn't that fascinating? She doesn't seem to be an herbivore after all. She's an everything-ivore. She's a give-me-all-your-dragon-food-right-now eater.

I wish I could take her out of the cage. I don't think she likes it. She limps around it, poking the bars and making this very dragony frown face. But I'm afraid if I did take her out, she would run away and get eaten or squashed.

She did a really funny thing, though. I had put the cage on my desk while I was reading (OK, I wasn't reading, I was thinking about the bleak unfairness of the dark universe and the death of love and hope), and when I came back to check on her, she had reached through the bars, grabbed a quill, and used it to drag one of my clean ink cloths over to the cage. Then she pulled the cloth through the bars and arranged it into a little nest on the floor of the cage.

Isn't that *amazing*?

My pet scavenger is a genius.

A genius who likes soft fluffy things, apparently, because I gave her some pin-cushions and other scraps of fabric (trying to get my ink cloth back, which did not work), and she ended up covering the entire bottom of the cage in them, basically a carpet, with a mountain of tiny pillows in the middle to sleep on.

I can make her better pillows! And a cozier nest! That will be my task for tomorrow. I can do that *and* think about how I will never love again at the same time.

She does look much more comfortable now. I think she was making a noise almost like singing earlier, before she fell asleep. Best little scavenger ever.

Good night, Stabby.

❀❀❀❀❀❀❀❀❀❀❀❀❀❀❀❀❀❀❀ DAY 4 ❀❀❀❀❀❀❀❀❀❀❀❀❀❀❀❀❀❀❀

Stabby spent most of today lying in her new nest, watching me and resting her injured foot. I hope it is not too badly injured, because I have no idea how to fix a scavenger paw, and when I tried to take her to the healers, they chased me off yelling about how they are not VETS and they only heal DRAGONS. RUDE.

I made Stabby some pillows stuffed with fur and I also cut up an old blanket, and she loved them, I think. At least, the squeaking sounded more delighted than furious this time, but I'm only guessing.

I also gave her some berries and honey and a bit of tortilla this morning, and she ate it all so fast that I tried offering her another dead mouse. SO MUCH YABBER-YELLING. Not going to try that again.

Blister came slinking by to ask who I would support for queen, which was such a weird question, because it's not up to me, is it? I know there are endless councils and debates happening right now, but surely, eventually Burn and Blister will fight and then one of them will win and that's our queen.

When I said something like that, she hmmmed and gave Stabby a sinister, tongue-flicker look, and then she slithered away again.

I think I'd better keep Stabby with me at all times.

✦✦✦✦✦✦✦✦✦✦✦✦✦✦✦✦✦✦✦ **DAY 5** ✦✦✦✦✦✦✦✦✦✦✦✦✦✦✦✦✦✦✦

This morning we had a visit from Blaze, who wanted to know if I would support *her* for queen, and I just barely managed not to laugh out loud. I had kind of forgotten that she was even an option. But I tried to tell her nicely that I didn't care who became the next queen, and then she pouted and complained for a while about all the beautiful missing treasure and how unfair it was that scavengers had stolen all of it before she even got to wear the best jewels. She kept side-eyeing Stabby, who was busy splashing around (I've given her two bowls of water now, since she apparently likes to have one to climb into and one to drink).

So I think that's yet another sister I need to protect Stabby from. This poor little scavenger, with only sad, tired me to watch out for her.

I wish I could guess what she's thinking. Her sweet huge eyes follow me all the time like she thinks I'm perfectly fascinating. Fascinating staring out the window, fascinating sighing at the ceiling, fascinating sobbing into my pillows. It does sort of make me want to do something more interesting so I can be half as fascinating as she thinks I am.

My scroll on pets has a chapter on fresh air and exercise ("Your pet puma will probably need to run around outside for a while! But your pet tortoise probably won't, ha ha!"), so I took Stabby's cage to the top of one of the courtyard towers for some of the afternoon. She watched all the dragons flying around us, her little head cocking side to side like an owl.

It was so peaceful up there with the wind and sunshine and spiraling flights of sand-colored dragons. I can't remember the last time I just sat and breathed and didn't feel like Mother was about to charge around a corner to roar at me. It's never been safe to stay still in this palace before, not when she was constantly roaming around, ready to spit fury at whomever she caught loafing.

Stabby actually clapped her little paws at the sunset, so we stayed and watched that, and then there was a funeral gathering of soldiers singing farewells to Queen Oasis, so we stayed up in the tower to listen to that, too. The cutest thing is that she made some noises like she wanted to sing along to the melody — isn't that wild? I never knew scavengers were little mimic songbirds like that.

Then the stars came out, and we were both very tired.

I'm sleeping with my tail curled around the birdcage tonight, just in case any of my sisters sneak in and try to get her while my eyes are closed. I will not feel the least bit bad about stabbing any of them with my tail if they try!

Good night, Stabby.

Today I spent the whole day making a little leash and a bell for Stabby so I can take her out of the cage. Six-Claws sent me to Dune, who laughed at me but agreed to help. We found leather we could cut to the right size, and made it soft and punched holes in it, and finally, late in the afternoon, I managed to trick Stabby into stepping into it so I could quick-smart tighten it around her middle.

She yelled a LOT, and she did not seem at all pleased when I used it to lift her out of the cage, although personally I thought it was really cute watching her flail around and shake her paws at me.

The hardest part was actually getting the bell on her. I'd attached it to a little armband, but even with Dune's help, I couldn't get her to keep it on; she kept pulling it right off and throwing it at me. Eventually I attached it to the leash, plunked her on my shoulder, and jumped out the window.

I figured finding herself in midair might stop the yelling, and it did! It totally worked! She went completely silent, grabbed my shoulder scales, and hung on tight. I flew her out into the desert, way up into the sky, above the clouds and along the currents and through the flickers of sunlight and shadow.

And somewhere along the way, I realized something. I survived Mother. I outlasted her. She could have gotten rid of me any moment of my life, and nearly did a few times, but now I was free, and I didn't have to be scared of her anymore.

And no matter what happened to Palm, wherever she was, I knew what she'd want for me: to keep living. To live every day like it was a victory.

I think she'd like my little scavenger.

When we got back, I held my talon up near my shoulder, and Stabby climbed onto it in a cute wobbly way. As I set her down inside her cage, she suddenly grabbed one of my claws and . . . this is going to sound weird, but she kind of hugged it? I'm sure scavengers don't know what hugging is, but that's what it felt like. Her two tiny arms wrapped around my claw for a moment, and I had this weird feeling that maybe she almost liked me, maybe even almost as much as I like her.

Was it because of the flying? I'll have to take her flying again and see if that's what makes her happy.

Anyway. It was a pretty nice day.

Good night, Stabby.

✸✸✸✸✸✸✸✸✸✸✸✸✸✸✸✸✸✸✸✸ DAY 7 ✸✸✸✸✸✸✸✸✸✸✸✸✸✸✸✸✸✸✸✸

My scavenger has a new name. I was walking her around the palace today (on her leash, on my shoulder), and she was making the most adorable squeaky-warble noises at everything. Dragons kept stopping to look at her and ask questions (like "Did that one kill Queen Oasis all by itself?" and "Are they all that small?" and "When are you going to eat it?") (it's a good thing my poor little pet can't understand them!).

I took her to the history museum, and we were wandering through the section where we keep old gifts from previous alliances with other tribes. Suddenly she started banging on my neck scales and squeaking at top volume and pointing at one of the walls. I took her over there, even though all I could see was a tapestry woven with images of different flowers — a gift from the SkyWing tribe a long time ago, I think.

The scavenger leaned way over, reaching for the tapestry, so I lifted her into my talons and brought her closer. She pointed to one of the flowers, then pointed to herself and squeaked.

"You want a flower?" I asked.

She did it again: point to flower, point to herself, squeak.

"You want to . . . eat a flower?" I squinted at her as she waved her paws all around herself, then pointed at the flower again, even more vigorously.

"Maybe you really like flowers," I guessed. "I could call you Flower — you seem a bit more like a Flower than a Stabby, actually. But that's not what you're saying, is it? That your name is Flower?" I thought about that for a moment. Surely it wasn't possible for a scavenger to name itself. That would imply that all those squeaks were a whole scavenger language, and that they had their own words for things, and a concept of themselves as separate individuals with names.

All right, too hilarious, Smolder. Clearly I am spending too much time with my scavenger if I was starting to imagine it could think like a dragon!

But I like the name Flower. *Stabby* was a name that would remind everyone about what happened to Mother. But surely none of the other dragons in the stronghold could be afraid of a cute little pet named Flower. Right?

Smolder and Flower. Flower and Smolder. That sounds OK to me.

Flower, I promise I'm going to take care of you. I'm going to protect you from dragons like Mother, the way I couldn't protect Palm. Whatever I have to do to stay alive, so you'll be safe, I'll do it.

We're going to be all right, you and me.

Good night, Flower.

CHAPTER 6
ICEWINGS

QUEEN GLACIER
AND THE GIFT OF LIGHT

ICEWINGS

SCALES: silvery scales like the moon or pale blue like ice

EYES: icy blue or dark blue

UNUSUAL CHARACTERISTICS: ridged claws to grip the ice; forked blue tongues; tails narrow to a whip-thin end

ABILITIES: can withstand subzero temperatures and bright light; exhale a deadly freezing breath

HABITAT: the icy arctic of the upper northwest peninsula, in snow caves and ice palaces

DIET: polar bears, fish, seals, walruses

QUEEN: Queen Snowfall

Starflight,

You know, IceWings have our own "Guide to the Dragons of Pyrrhia" for our dragonets. It's like the NightWing one that's so popular everywhere else, only ours is obviously better! Here's an excerpt:

SkyWings are red

SeaWings are blue

Don't trust anyone

Who looks different from you

RainWings change color

MudWings are brown

If a dragon's not an IceWing

They're a danger to our crown

NightWings are black

SandWings are beige

If you see someone unfamiliar

You should immediately ice them in the face just to be safe

Hmmm. So yes, all right, maybe ours needs updating as well. What a WILD idea to actually ask all the tribes for their own documents and stories! We certainly have plenty of those in the palace, but I also cast a wider net and asked for submissions from the outer villages, too. See, I have become a queen who is interested in new perspectives from ALL OVER THE PLACE. You are welcome.

I also put together a partial list of our tribe's gifts from animus dragons in centuries past, in case that's of interest.

Please send me a copy of the guide when it's done.

On the winds of blizzards,
Queen Snowfall

P.S. My sister Mink asked that I send you her application to Jade Mountain Academy. I'm not saying she should get special consideration because she's my sister, but I am *the queen.*

Dear very important dragons at the best school in Pyrrhia,

My name is Mink and I am an IceWing princess and I am two years old and I would really really really really really really really really really like to come be a student at Jade Mountain Academy, please please.

~~My cousin Winter says it is really fun there and that everyone is really nice.~~ Oh. All right, my sister says I should only write completely totally true things, so I guess maybe what he actually said was: "Oh yes, *you* would fit right in, Mink." But doesn't that sound nice? I like fitting in places! Once I fit inside an igloo my friend Polar Bear made that was so small no one else could fit into it except me. It was really great except for the part where I couldn't get out again and everyone had to carefully cut apart the igloo to save me and it took like a whole day. Which was so nice of them, though, and Polar Bear wasn't even mad.

Snowfall says maybe I should tell you about why IceWings are so awesome and maybe you could put it in your book! That would be very very exciting and a little scary, to see my words in a scroll that everyone and everyone could read in all the whole world.

I love being an IceWing because my mother was the best queen in the world and now my sister is also the best queen in the world, and no other tribe has had two amazing queens in a row like that. My mother, Queen Glacier, cared about everyone in the tribe and made lots of important decisions and still had time to snuggle with me. She was smart and fair, and she took care of that funny silly SandWing princess who had to run away from her sisters, even though that princess was really *exceptionably* silly.

I also love being an IceWing because we have lots and lots of school so we know lots and LOTS of things! I am so great at labeling maps! And copying scrolls really neatly! And memorizing lists of queens! And catching fish and seals! But my favorite subject is art and I am really amazing at ice sculpture and I will send you a piece of my art so you can see how hard I work on it and also how much I love you. (This is a sculpture of my pet arctic fox who I named Snowy after my sister.) (Snowfall says it will definitely melt by the time it gets there, which I don't know much about because I haven't left the Ice Kingdom very much. But maybe it won't! She says she'll fill a box with ice and frostbreath and see if that helps, so I am going to hope very hopefully that you get my sculpture and love it, too!)

IceWings work really hard and try really hard to be the best at whatever they love. We also have really amazing parties and talent shows and competitions. There are always new recipes and scrolls and songs and jewelry because everyone is trying so hard to make something wonderful, and everything they create, they share with the tribe. I love visiting my friends to see what they're working on. Maybe sometimes I wish we made more stuff together instead of everyone in their own room making something alone, but I think my sister is going to change that (and if she doesn't, I will tell her to!).

The most important thing you should know about me is that I love love love school and I would be really excited to go to a school that is school all the time but also mostly about making friends because the thing I love even more than school is friends. When Winter said Jade Mountain Academy was "basically a school where all you learn is hugging and friendship" I got SO EXCITED because those are my FAVORITE THINGS and I want to learn about them all day long!

I think I would be really really really really really good at making friends with other tribes. Mother said one way to make friends is to ask other dragons questions about themselves, and I have *so many* questions! Like, don't SandWings accidentally bop their own faces with their tails all the time? I whack my snout with my tail about a trillion million times a day, and every time I think, whew, imagine if that had venom in it! I would be so dead! Also, if RainWings can choose what color they are, why don't they choose to look like IceWings all the time? Do they know that white and blue are the prettiest colors? Also, what kinds of pets do SeaWings have? Pufferfish? Squids? Little tiny seahorses? Does anyone have a pet walrus? What about a pet seal? I know we eat them all the time but I kind of think they are really cute and maybe I would like to have one be my friend? And so I wondered if a SeaWing has ever done that and if seals are as cuddly as they look. See, I just want to ask everyone questions all day long! And so that means everyone would like me and want to be my friend, right?

Those are all the reasons I hope you will let me come be a student at Jade Mountain Academy, and I promise I will be really good and learn lots of things and love everybody and you will be really happy I'm there!

Snow mountains of love,
Mink

Unfortunately Mink's sculpture melted soon after it arrived, but one of our students drew this picture for us first.
— Starflight

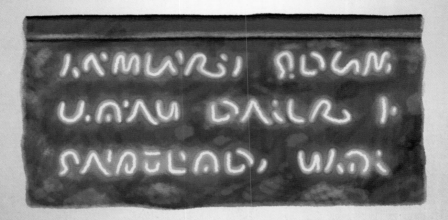

I am enclosing this piece of the rankings wall for the Jade Mountain
Academy museum so your students can study it.

– Queen Snowfall

THE ANIMUS GIFTS OF THE ICEWINGS

WITH NOTATIONS BY QUEEN SNOWFALL

- The gift of defense (also known as the Great Ice Cliff)
  Currently under destruction.

- The gift of splendor (also known as the IceWing palace)
  Created by a pair of animus twins who designed the whole vast palace and enchanted it so the impenetrable walls would never crack or melt.

- The gift of light (also known as the tree of light and its moon globes)
  Created by Frostbite, who sculpted it with her own claws before enchanting it, and it astonishingly looks like a real tree, which I know now that I've seen real trees.

- The gift of order (also known as the rankings wall)
  A torturous method of establishing a hierarchy among the IceWing aristocracy, designed to make dragons compete and dislike each other. Destroyed by me! Good riddance.

- The gift of elegance (also known as the pale blue snowflakes in the ice walls of the palace)

  These change to reflect the weather outside. So that we can . . . tell if it's snowing without walking over to a window? Seems RATHER pointless. Well, some dragons think they're pretty.

- The gift of subsistence (three holes in the ice located on the outskirts of the kingdom where IceWings can reach into the ocean and always pull out a seal)

  This is one of those gifts I understand better now that I'm a queen and responsible for the health of all my subjects.

- The gift of healing (five narwhal horns enchanted to cure frostbreath injuries)

  I believe Queen Diamond was hit with a blast of frostbreath when she was a dragonet or something, which is why she chose to create these for her gift. They are certainly useful when there are accidents in training or at the schools, but could have been much more useful if they cured other injuries as well, such as those one might incur during wars with other tribes. I mean, seriously. Then again, these are an absolute delight compared to her unofficial gift of a crown that makes the wearer hate NightWings, and her other unofficial gift of the terrible Trial secret in the Diamond Caves (don't ask questions; that's all we're going to say on the matter).

- The gift of diplomacy (three bracelets that keep non-IceWing guests warm and let them travel safely over the Great Ice Cliff)

  Created thousands of years ago by a dragon named Penguin, who really should've made more than three.

- The gift of strength (tiara)

  Very useful, but definitely worth paying attention to the reminder to use cautiously.

- The gift of compromise (a scepter carved from a dark blue rock with little diamonds in it)

  I haven't tried using this yet, since obviously I am excellent at working out compromises without any magical help.

- The gift of vision (an opal ring)

  Offers annoying but useful visions courtesy of an animus named Opal.

- The gift of stealth (pale silver wristbands set with diamonds)

  Very useful for sneaking up on ~~enemies~~ new friends.

- "Part of" the gift of understanding (an unwearable mystery piece of silver)

  I have no understanding yet of what this is or why we only have part of it. VERY ANNOYING.

I found this in my mother's library and thought you might be interested. Most IceWing feasts aren't this fancy or long, and I certainly didn't get an elaborate coronation feast like this, given that the tribe was in mourning. But it'll give you an idea of some IceWing delicacies, as I have eaten most of these foods in some form or another.

— Queen Snowfall

A ROYAL FEAST
FOR THE CORONATION OF HER MAJESTY QUEEN GLACIER

Revise according to my notes! — Queen Glacier

1ST COURSE

A light salad of kelp and sedge
garnished with garlic and ginger

Delicious!

2ND COURSE

A cool crab soup, delicately
flavored with moss

3RD COURSE

Thinly shaved whale skin topped
with polar bear meat

4TH COURSE

Narwhal blubber seasoned
with fulmar oil

Igloo, I know you are the best chef in the kingdom, but have you actually ever tasted oil from a fulmar? Those birds have a mean streak and the only thing worse than getting their oil in your mouth is getting it in your eyes!

>>>>>>>>>⌒ 5TH COURSE ⌒<<<<<<<<<

A hearty cold stew of diced puffin breast
and grated gannet stomach

You know, we could skip the courses and just have a buffet and everyone could mix and match their meats . . .

>>>>>>>>>⌒ 6TH COURSE ⌒<<<<<<<<<

Sliced scavenger liver

Igloo. Yuck. No.

>>>>>>>>>⌒ 7TH COURSE ⌒<<<<<<<<<

A carving of shark heart

I know there's some old tale about getting strength from eating the heart of a shark, but I've also seen many an IceWing get sick after having shark, so I'm going to say no on this one.

>>>>>>>>>⌒ DESSERT ⌒<<<<<<<<<

Shaved ice flavored with syrup from maple trees
or lemons traded from the SkyWings

OR

Frozen cream with melon
A rare MudWing delicacy, made from
the milk of the royal cowherd and melons
from the edge of the rainforest

IN THE
VILLAGE-OF-THE-PLENTIFUL-SEALS

BY CARIBOU THE ICEWING

It is strange to be asked to write something for a scroll that will be published by an academy and shared with readers of every tribe. I do not believe anyone in the outer IceWing villages has ever been invited to do anything like this. We have writers, of course, but our scrolls are usually written on sealskin and circulate from village to village only in the Ice Kingdom, carried by wandering librarians.

We also have revered storytellers who sing the tales of the Great Ice Dragon and the long history of the IceWing tribe and all the stories of our heroes. But they don't have to write anything down; they recite it all from memory. Dragonets are chosen to be the next bards of their village based on their memory and performance skills. It is every young dragon's dream to be one of them. I remember dreaming of it myself, once.

I should introduce myself; that is often where the bards begin when they perform. I am the Caribou of my generation, not to be confused with my mother, Caribou, or my grandmother Caribou. Also not to be confused with my friend Caribou or my other

friend's sister Caribou or any of the other dragons named Caribou in our village. There is always one in each family, usually more. We carry the name to honor the animus princess who gave us the gift of subsistence many centuries ago.

In retrospect, I can see that it might have been simpler to rename the village after her, like We-Remember-and-Venerate-Caribou did. That would probably have been less confusing.

But I think Village-of-the-Plentiful-Seals is a better name! And I like being called Caribou after her; it makes me feel special, even though there are about thirty of us in the village right now.

Where-No-Dragon-Goes-Hungry went the statue route to honor her instead. It's not even made of ice; it's carved from a giant whale bone, I believe, and it stands in the center of their village with its talons outstretched like it's blessing them. They even traded some of their seals (probably a LOT of seals) to get sapphires for her eyes. Every year they have a Caribou celebration where dragons compete to make the best ice sculpture of her, and for months there are Caribous of ice scattered all throughout their village.

Our Caribou celebration is a yearly feast where we invite every IceWing in the outer villages to come eat, sing, tell stories, dance, and eat some more for five days and nights under the three moons and the shimmering green-gold-pale aurora borealis of the Great Ice Dragon's frostbreath.

We-Remember-and-Venerate-Caribou has a market instead that runs all year long, where every dragon in the Ice Kingdom knows they can trade for food. Or if they have nothing to trade and they're starving, they can go to the temple of the Great Ice Dragon and they'll be fed for free. (We have one of those, too, of course!)

Should I explain the gift of subsistence? It is a hole in the ice where any dragon can reach in and pull out a seal to eat, every time. Princess Caribou made three: one for a village on the northeast coast (We-Remember-and-Venerate-Caribou), one for a village on the southwestern tip of the kingdom (Where-No-Dragon-Goes-Hungry), and one for a village in the southeast, the farthest distance from the queen's palace (that's us!).

Our legends say that there was a great uproar when the princess unveiled her gift. The IceWing aristocracy could not begin to fathom an animus gift that was intended for dragons outside their circles. Something that kept lowly villagers alive instead of a trinket that made noble scales shinier?! What was Princess Caribou thinking?!

They all muttered that it would make us lazy. That we would forget how to hunt or look after ourselves. That lowly dragons needed to be hungry so we would be motivated to work harder. That free seals meant we would lie around eating all day, neglect our dragonets, abandon our studies, and turn into snoozy, slack-jawed walruses.

But there was nothing they could do. Caribou wisely made her gift before sharing it with anyone, so it was done, and even if her family raged at her, they couldn't change it. One gift was all any animus dragon could give.

And guess what? All those snooty royal dragons were wrong. We are not lazy walruses. We are thriving, happy villagers. No one has to worry about going hungry, so everyone is safe and free. Our teachers can focus on being the greatest teachers in Pyrrhia, instead of spending half their days hunting or starving. Our chefs are the most creative, and our hunters can go far afield and try new techniques to catch unusual prey, knowing we'll survive even if they sometimes come back with empty claws. Our warriors are strong and our architects are brilliant. All our dragonets are happy and healthy, because parents have time to spend with them and never have to fear for their survival.

Besides which, everyone in the village has time for what they love to do. Some dragons love hunting, and they can go ahead and do that. But many dragons love to write, or sing, or sculpt, or run scientific experiments, or build, and with the strength from the free seals, they can create art all day long if they want to.

Personally, I think life is better out here than in the palace. The nobles think it must be so miserable to live in an outer village, but with the gift of subsistence, we can live such joyous, peaceful lives. (Or at least, we can when we're not being called up to war, or felled by a mysterious plague. I am glad *someone* remembered to bring us the magic earrings that saved us from that — I'm sure there are queens and nobles throughout IceWing history who would have forgotten we needed them at all!) (And it was pretty fascinating to meet Prince Winter. He was quite different from how I imagined the royal family.)

There's one more piece of the legend of Princess Caribou that might be interesting for your scroll. In our songs and odes, we tell of her kindness, her empathy, her vision and compassion. But one poem also tells of the friend who brought her to our villages in the first place.

Every year, a few bright dragonets from the outer villages are invited to the palace for a chance to compete for a spot in the palace school. If they make it in, and they work hard and do well, they have a chance to enter the circles and rise into the nobility. That is how Princess Caribou met an ordinary outer villager named Snowstorm, who became her best friend and eventually her closest advisor. As the story goes, he brought her to our villages and showed her what life was really like for dragons outside the palace.

We believe he inspired the gift of subsistence, and that is why my brother is named Snowstorm, and so is my father, and so are another twenty or so dragons in the village, and listen, it's not the least confusing situation, but on the plus side, we rarely have to stress about forgetting someone's name!

Of course, We-Remember-and-Venerate-Caribou and Where-No-Dragon-Goes-Hungry both think Snowstorm originally lived in their villages, but they're wrong. He was definitely from Village-of-the-Plentiful-Seals, the best and happiest village in the Ice Kingdom.

And next year my daughter Caribou is going to attend the Jade Mountain Academy, and maybe she will meet a royal IceWing there (or a dragon from another tribe altogether!). Maybe she'll show that royal how brilliant an outer villager can be, and maybe they'll become best friends, and they'll change something else about the future of the IceWings, or even the whole continent.

Anything is possible, right?

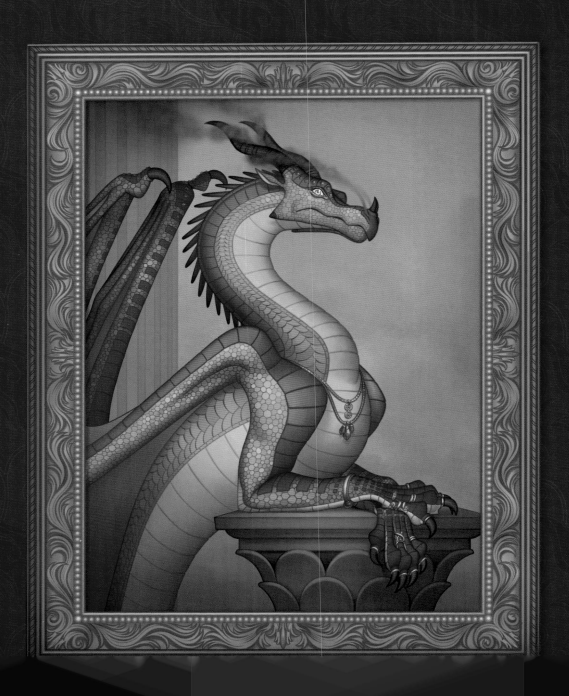

CHAPTER 7
SKYWINGS

QUEEN SCARLET
PORTRAIT IN THE WINGERY

SKYWINGS

SCALES: red/gold or orange

EYES: orange, amber, or yellow

UNUSUAL CHARACTERISTICS: enormous wings

ABILITIES: powerful fighters and fliers; can breathe fire

HABITAT: high in the Claws of the Clouds Mountains,
in caves and spires and palaces carved out of rock

DIET: mountain goats, cougars, squirrels, rabbits, birds of prey

QUEEN: Queen Ruby

Starflight —

Among my mother's things I found this very creepy and cryptic list of her enemies and her reasons for hating them — and since she crossed a bunch of names off and a lot of those dragons are dead, I think these were probably the scores she wanted to settle. The scroll, as you can see, is tattered, and some of the ink is quite old, but a few of the entries are fresh. I think she must have had this with her while she was on the run. I can easily imagine her reading and rereading it obsessively, plotting and planning.

— Vermilion

P.S. I have no record of a dragon named Beryl or why Mother would've hated them enough to put them on the list. I hope that whoever they are, they're safe now that she's gone.

~~Mother~~ – so much fun fighting her to the death, best day ever

~~Sister~~ – easy

~~Canyon~~ – what an enormous bore he turned out to be

Beryl – everything is ready, when the time is right

~~My Traitorous Daughter~~ – can't live without her but won't live with her, ha; if only I could live forever

~~Brightest Night Eggs~~ – no more tiny SkyWing heroes for the prophecy, what a shame

~~Kestrel~~ – I probably should thank her for Peril before I kill her

Update: very annoying that apparently someone killed her before I could

~~Osprey~~ – disloyal, weak, useless; at least killing him was thrilling

The Dragonets of Destiny – who needs them, really?

Glory – that sneaky viper of a RainWing, I can't believe she's queen of two tribes when I've lost my throne; I'm going to rip her head off next time I see her

~~Burn~~ – too slippery for her own good, wouldn't even fight for her throne like a real queen, got what she deserved after trying to lock me up

Smolder – "just following orders" my tail, when I get my claws on you, you'll be sorry, you and your little scavenger, too

Chameleon – so annoying and only barely helpful; time to figure out his secrets and get rid of him

Vermilion – suddenly disobedient when I'm not right in front of him! What a snake, princes are the worst

Peril – ungrateful untrustworthy backstabber

Wow, Glory, we always knew she hated you but this is so . . . descriptive! I think she hated you the mostest. Congratulations!
— Tsunami

You know, I'm just honored to have made the list. — Glory

Starflight,

I found the following documents to send over for your project: a letter from Queen Carmine from almost two thousand years ago, and a scroll about a SkyWing tradition from before my mother's time; possibly even from before my grandmother's time. I'm thinking about reviving this idea but tweaking some of the challenges. Anyway, both of them seemed musty and ancient, so I figured you'd like them.

Also, I know you asked for an essay on the best qualities of the SkyWing tribe, but I think what I am sending is mucah more interesting and delightful, and I'm sure you will, too: our tribe's new anthem, written by my darling genius son, Prince Cliff. I think you'll agree that it's the best song ever written in the history of the world. Best of luck to the other tribes who will now start trying to write their own anthems! Ha!

— Queen Ruby

Queen Pearl,

Your note of condolence on the death of my daughter Princess Sunset left something to be desired, especially considering your uncle killed her and your own mother's negligence is why she's dead. You had better fulfill your promise of five years of tribute in gems, as well as your promise to remove your SeaWings from the villages you built in our territory and never encroach on our land again.

Eagle tells me in exchange that I can't mention this horrific massacre — and how precarious things are in your kingdom — to anyone. Fine. For now, I'll tell my SkyWings that Princess Sunset died in a terrible accident. I expect your secret will be known halfway across Pyrrhia before long. These kinds of stories get out, you know.

And when the story spreads, all of Pyrrhia will see how wise our tribe is to dispose of soulless creatures like animus dragons or firescales before they can harm anyone. As soon as our dragonets can speak, we set them in front of a small fire and have them tell it to go out. If it does, we aren't foolish enough to let them live, let alone to place them in a position of power.

I understand you have outlawed animus magic in your kingdom. I also know that your brother, Fathom, is an animus and still alive. This is dangerous. From one queen to another, let me advise you that sometimes we have to make difficult decisions on behalf of our tribes. I urge you to make the right choice now, before another tragedy bloodies your beaches. It's your duty — in memory of your family, and of mine.

— Queen Carmine

CLASH OF CLAWS TOURNAMENT

Every seven years, SkyWings from across the kingdom gather at the palace to compete in the Clash of Claws. This weeklong test of strength, endurance, and cleverness draws brave dragons who seek to prove themselves to their queen, tribe, and kingdom. Their reward? Glory, fame, and a seat at the queen's table of advisors.

Seven days, seven challenges.

FLAME: All aspects of a competitor's fire are tested, from precision of use to intensity and heat of the flame.

ENDURANCE: A token is left for each competitor at the top of the tallest mountain in the kingdom. Dragons must race from the palace to the top of the mountain, testing their speed, stamina, and ability to withstand the cold.

STRENGTH: Heavy boulders are brought from the Diamond Spray River. Each competitor must fly as high up as possible while carrying their boulder and then throw the boulder as far as they can.

CUNNING: Elaborate mazes with secret rooms are constructed, full of dazzling treasures that competitors must acquire — if they can survive the snares and traps laid throughout.

GUILE: Each competitor must find a scavenger, that cleverest of prey, and bring them back to the palace — alive and unharmed.

WIT: Each competitor must answer correctly a series of riddles crafted by the queen and her advisors.

SPEED: A straightforward flying race to determine who is the fastest dragon in the fastest tribe!

SKYWING ANTHEM
BY PRINCE CLIFF OF THE SKYWINGS

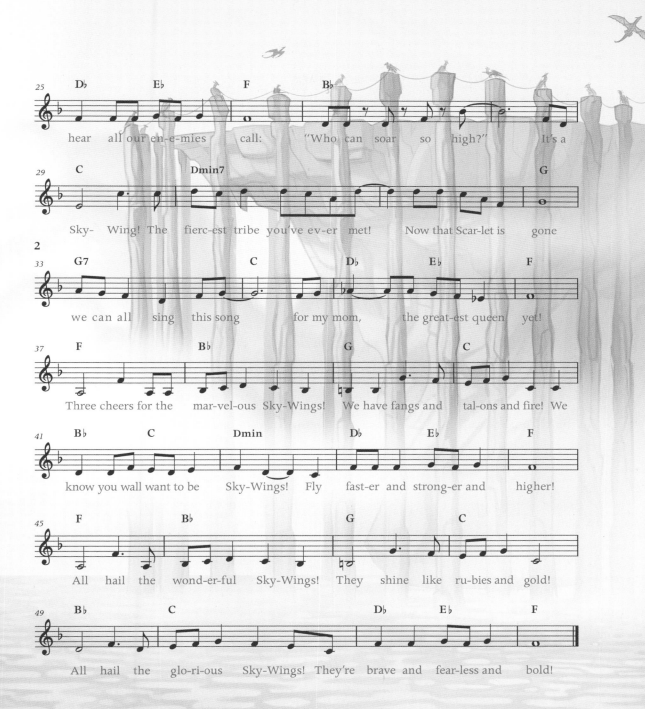

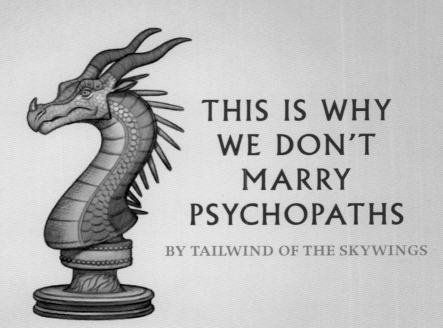

THIS IS WHY WE DON'T MARRY PSYCHOPATHS

BY TAILWIND OF THE SKYWINGS

Listen, I'm old enough to remember Princess Scarlet as a baby dragonet, and she was the *worst*. The very first thing she learned to do was point at things and scream until someone gave them to her. Then she learned that if she screamed for no reason, dragons would come running and give her random things to make her stop, so she would do that just to see what she could get. She screamed anytime she didn't get her way, and I'm talking about the highest-pitched angry-eagle shriek you've ever heard. The whole palace echoed with her rage basically from the moment she hatched.

Also, she stole treasure from every single dragon in the palace. Just sauntered into their rooms snatching jewelry, or breaking their treasure chests to rifle through them. When anyone confronted her about it, she would stare at them as though they were speaking some weird scavenger language she'd never heard before. She could be *wearing* the very necklace they accused her of stealing, and she would still act as though they were absolutely incomprehensible.

Her mother did nothing to stop her, of course. Queen Firestorm thought Scarlet was *terribly* funny. The more vicious or cruel or dramatic she was, the more Firestorm would laugh. She was constantly comparing her daughters to one another: who's the prettiest, who's the cleverest, who played the meanest prank on the court. Who said the most bitingly awful thing about someone else, preferably to their face.

Firestorm believed all dragons were just as nasty on the inside as she was, so she prided herself on "being honest" with everyone, especially her dragonets. "I'm *helping* you," she would explain airily. "If you don't *know* your face looks like it was smashed into a wall, you *should*."

In those days, the arena was used mainly for parades, art shows, dance performances, and beauty contests. Queen Firestorm would have dragons come from all over Pyrrhia to compete, and then she would keep the winning sculptures or tapestries for her own palace. I don't know what happened to all that fancy art. Over her thirty-year reign, Scarlet replaced almost all of it with statues of herself.

Scarlet was lucky that she measured up to her mother's standards of beauty. Her youngest sister was exiled to one of the northern outposts at the age of three, simply because her looks offended Firestorm. Only beautiful dragons were allowed in the queen's throne room, and sometimes Firestorm would stroll through the wingery just to snark about the least attractive dragonets.

It's kind of a miracle *I* didn't get kicked out of the palace in those years. I have no idea what looks pretty or doesn't. I don't care about arranging my jewels just right or matching my rings with my eyes or whatever the fashion is. I like making strong, practical swords and then hitting bad guys with them. My one useful skill was probably staying out of Queen Firestorm's way.

Once, I was brought in to teach an ironsmithing class while Scarlet was still in the wingery. That day was enough for me to quit teaching forever. Imagine trying to talk about metal and fire while a sneering dragonet scoffs at your ragged claws, distracts everyone else by talking nonstop about her hatching day party, and shrieks every time a spark comes anywhere near her.

Yeah. She was not my favorite.

So a few years later, when my brother told me he had set his sights on her, I laughed in his face.

"What?" Canyon snapped, bristling. "We're a noble family! We've married royals before! And I'm extremely handsome! Look at this jawline! I polish my scales every day! I could easily marry Princess Scarlet!"

"If you want to be miserable your whole life and die young, sure," I agreed.

"Why would I be miserable?" he demanded. "She'll probably be the next queen! That would make me king!"

"Right — until she gets bored of you and kills you," I pointed out.

"She won't," he said huffily. "She will be too madly in love with me!"

I laughed so hard I nearly fell off the balcony. He had stomped off in a fury by the time I caught my breath.

I didn't chase him down. I assumed this fleeting madness would pass. There was nothing to love about Scarlet. She was so obviously *awful*.

And to be quite honest, there wasn't much to love about Canyon either. He was shamelessly obsessed with his looks. If he had spent as much time on any task as he did on his scale-polishing and muscle-building, he might have been quite a successful dragon. As it was, he had almost nothing to talk about except himself, and yet he still boringly dominated every conversation because he thought he was smarter than everyone about everything.

Listen, I'm not the sentimental sort. Sorry if you expected more of a heartfelt tale of woe about my poor stupid brother. He was really only a dragon I happened to be related to.

When I was growing up, families weren't about love and cuddling. Nobody carried their dragonet around with them everywhere the way Queen Ruby does with Prince Cliff. Sometimes I see her chatting with him for *hours*, and I cannot begin to fathom what they could be talking about. (I'll admit Cliff is more entertaining than your average dragonet, but dragonets in general are so dull!)

No, we had a normal SkyWing family — a normal pre-Scarlet SkyWing family, that is. Mother and Father could have chosen partners for themselves, but they were busy, so they put their names on a list and let Queen Firestorm match them up. They liked each other well enough to get married. Weddings were still quiet ceremonies in the clouds back then, just the two marrying dragons saying a few ritual words to each other in the open sky.

During Scarlet's reign, weddings became another excuse for a party, and every party was an excuse for a brutal day in her murder stadium. Nobody could get married without at least three violent death matches first. Most dragons decided it wasn't worth the trouble (or the cleanup). Some probably snuck away to do their own ceremonies in the sky, but they didn't record them in the SkyWing Ancestry Scrolls. Most dragons also didn't want to let Scarlet choose their matches for them, so many of them chose no one at all.

But back to Mother and Father: like normal SkyWing parents, they hatched me and Canyon, kept us alive until we were old enough to hunt for ourselves, and then sent us off to find jobs in the palace. That's how it was done. I'm not even sure they stayed together after we left. We were all busy with our own things. It was only a coincidence that my rooms were next door to Canyon's; otherwise I might never have seen him except in passing.

That is, until he started appearing near the dais at every royal court function. He had finally, after years of trying, managed to make himself beautiful enough to catch Queen Firestorm's attention, and she added him to her little crowd of hangers-on. Which gave him a chance to be near Princess Scarlet.

I don't know how he did it, and frankly, I'm not sure I want to know how you get a self-absorbed psychopath to choose you as their one and only. He didn't even bother to tell me to my face. I heard about the engagement when it was announced from the throne, like everyone else in court.

And three MOONS, was he insufferable about it! Strutting around the palace, swishing his tail, flaunting his diamond ring at everyone, and always with the most dreadful smug face on. I did my best to avoid him, but he cornered me in the kitchen one day while I was inspecting the cauldrons.

"Did you hear?" he smarmed, flapping the talon with his engagement ring on it. "That *the* Princess Scarlet has chosen *me* to be her husband? I *told* you I could do it. You'd better be more polite to me from now on."

"Sure, Canyon," I said with a shrug. I was not about to be provoked into an argument with *her* fiancé. I knew I couldn't do anything to stop him, so at that point I was just calculating how much white silk I would have to buy for his funeral (he was big, so, a lot, I figured).

"I *assume* you'll come to the wedding," he snooted.

I gave him a funny look. "Your wedding? In the sky? You're planning on having guests?"

He cackled. "This is a ROYAL wedding, Tailwind. It's going to be the event of the season! Scarlet and I have been planning it for days. We'll have it in the arena, and we'll decorate with chains of rubies and flaming scavengers, and the feast will involve roasted elephants and seared leopards, and maybe there will be a pit full of gold coins for us to roll in."

"Sounds . . . extravagant," I said.

"*Everyone* who's *anyone* will be there," he said.

"Well, I guess I'm anyone, so see you there," I said.

"You'll see me," he said haughtily. "I will be far too busy and famous to see you." And off he swanned, adoring himself.

The wedding of Canyon and Princess Scarlet turned out to be even more extravagant and ridiculous than I imagined. It was also quite memorable, because, in the middle of it, Scarlet challenged her mother for the throne and, of course, won, so, that was messy. She went on to poison her older sister at the banquet (and several other dragons by accident as well). It was officially the deadliest day in the Sky Kingdom since the last war. By dawn the next morning, there were corpses everywhere, and Canyon looked rather more pale and shell-shocked than your average happy groom.

I did not make the mistake of interacting with him after that. My plan was to avoid this queen even more rigorously than I avoided the last one. The smithy was too hot and smelly for her, so it was an excellent place to hide myself away. I stayed there, cranking out nasty-looking swords and spears for her arena, plus whatever weird new prisoner traps she wanted, and that kept her happy enough to ignore me.

Then, of course, once we joined the War of SandWing Succession, there was plenty of work to do making weapons and armor and more weapons and more armor, for years upon years upon years.

She'd gotten rid of Canyon by then, though. He lasted much longer than I expected, honestly. A full twelve years — who would have guessed? Long enough to give her sixteen eggs: four males, twelve females. Plenty of heirs for Scarlet to toy with and then kill off, one by one.

Maybe he survived that long because she was busy dealing with the royal challenges from her two surviving sisters (nice try, obviously doomed, not sure why they didn't go throw themselves in the ocean as soon as she became queen instead), her first two daughters (why even bother before the age of twenty, I mean, really), and one niece (very stupid, she could have kept her head down and might have survived just fine, no idea what she was thinking).

But after twelve years, even Queen Scarlet had to notice what a giant egotistical troll was sitting on the throne beside her (and by "beside" I obviously mean "below"). I'm not sure what tipped her over the edge. Perhaps she noticed that he was ordering huge statues of himself to sit beside hers (all smashed now, no surprise). Perhaps he told her some earrings would look better on him than they did on her. Perhaps he was hogging the mirror one day when she wanted to look at herself.

Perhaps she just got bored of listening to him. Canyon was definitely dim enough to think he could give her advice or question her decisions. He probably got careless and let it slip that he thought he was smarter than her, or prettier.

Perhaps she also thought twelve heirs was quite sufficient, thank you.

There are lots of ways to offend a vain psychopath. But whatever he did, the end result was him on the sands of her arena, shaking with terror. Scarlet thought it was too, too thrilling: the king himself, fighting any challenger who volunteered (and if that didn't work, several prisoners who didn't)!

I didn't go to watch, although I did send him my best throwing knives and a set of mirrored armor I thought he would like. (Although I worried a bit that he'd get distracted by looking at his own face in it.) Didn't help, though. He lasted two fights (again, more than I would have guessed) and was killed in the third by a SkyWing general who probably hoped he could take Canyon's place as Scarlet's next husband. (Hilariously optimistic and staggeringly stupid; he was so lucky she wasn't even remotely interested in marrying again.)

Poor foolish Canyon. He never even saw Ruby hatch. I wonder what he would think if he could see his daughter now: queen of the SkyWings, and somehow, mysteriously, not evil at all. (Well, so far.) Maybe that would make him glance away from his mirror for a moment and go, "Huh. How did I manage to make something good, for once?"

All right, not very likely. He'd probably say something more like "Is *that* necklace *really* what you're planning on wearing? With your coloring?"

Ah, well. Looks like we'll have a proper SkyWing royal wedding soon, now that Queen Ruby thinks it's safe to marry Cliff's father and let everyone know who he is. My gold is on that kind-eyed caretaker who's always working in the wingery. I think his name is Jasper. He seems like a dragon who could be a good father — something Canyon was never interested in. Jasper doesn't look like he wastes his time on preening or treasure or fripperies. And he likes Ruby, who is levelheaded, not very murdery, and the least evil queen we've had in ages, so he must be reasonably smart.

Let's hope he lasts longer than any of our previous kings!

Tsetse Hive

Beetle Lake

Vinegaroon
Hive

Sinkhole

Hornet Hive

Cicada Hive

PANTALA

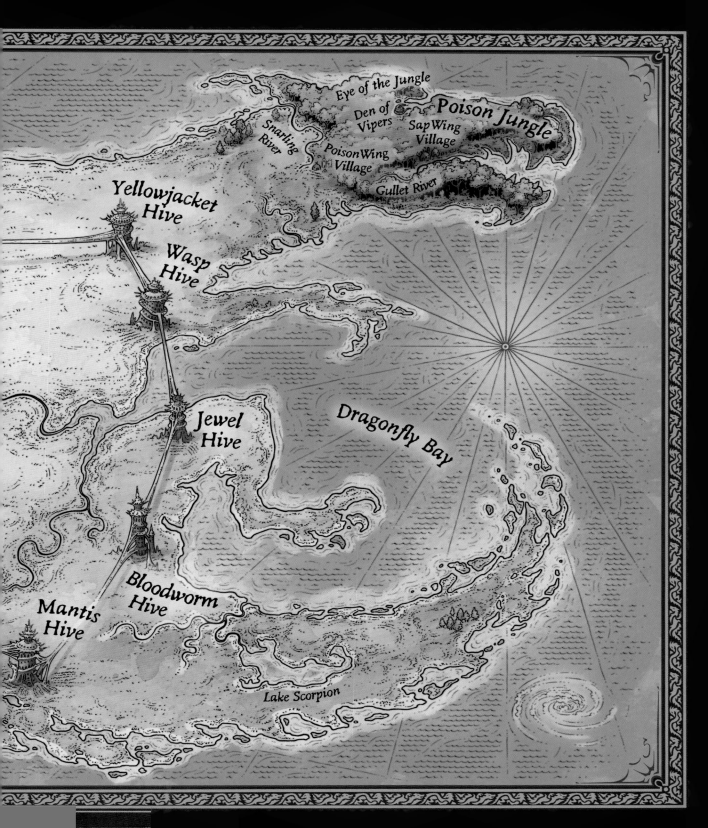

Eye of the Jungle

Poison Jungle

Den of Vipers

Sap Wing Village

Snarling River

Poison Wing Village

Gullet River

Yellowjacket Hive

Wasp Hive

Jewel Hive

Dragonfly Bay

Bloodworm Hive

Mantis Hive

Lake Scorpion

Hi Starflight!

I'm so fascinated by your book idea. Will there be extra copies for all the libraries of Pantala? I love to imagine dragons from all ten tribes learning about one another and reading each other's stories! Thank you for including all the Pantalan tribes; I hope all the material I gathered for you is helpful.

You know what you should do next? Add SilkWing, HiveWing, and LeafWing students to Jade Mountain Academy! Wouldn't that be amazing? I know it's a long way to go, but I'm sure we can find lots of interested dragonets. (I would send you Bumblebee, but we'll have to see if she's less of a handful once she's older. I don't want to exhaust all your teachers!)

And maybe one day we can start a school somewhere in between our continents, so it's more of an equal distance for everyone. What do you think?

Send me a message soon — I want to hear all about the book and the library and the scavengers and your experiments and your research and everything you've discovered since your last letter!

— Cricket

CHAPTER 8
SILKWINGS

QUEEN MONARCH
IN THE PANTALA FORESTS

Tsetse Hive

Yellowjacket Hive

Wasp Hive

Vinegaroon Hive

Sinkhole

Jewel Hive

Hornet Hive

Cicada Hive

Mantis Hive

Bloodworm Hive

SILKWINGS

SCALES: any color under the sun except black

EYES: any color

UNUSUAL CHARACTERISTICS: SilkWing dragonets are born wingless, but go through a metamorphosis at age six, when they spin a cocoon and emerge after five days with silk-spinning abilities and four huge wings that look much like butterfly wings; all SilkWings also have antennae

ABILITIES: can spin silk from glands on their wrists to create webs or other woven articles; can detect vibrations with their antennae to assess threats; some are born with "flamesilk," an ability to spin threads of fire

HABITAT: SilkWings are naturally tree dwellers who once lived in the vast forests of Pantala, but since the Tree Wars they have inhabited the webs that connect the Hives

DIET: vegetarians; these dragons prefer plant-based foods

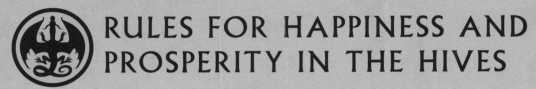

RULES FOR HAPPINESS AND PROSPERITY IN THE HIVES

BY IO OF THE SILKWINGS

Something other dragons should know about life as a SilkWing is that there are a *lot* of rules to follow. In theory, HiveWings have to follow rules, too, but there are way more rules for SilkWings.

Each Hive has a place like Misbehaver's Way in Cicada Hive, where dragons who dare to break the rules and ignore HiveWing restrictions are punished. Super-creepy HiveWing guards with special stingers paralyze these poor dragons and leave them on display on stone pedestals for entire days as a warning to other potential rulebreakers. SilkWing schools take their students to Misbehaver's Way twice a year, on "field trips," to terrify young dragonets into obedience. Do HiveWings dragonets get traumatized in this way? Nope.

Not all Hive rules are written down — some we just learn from our parents — but a lot of them are engraved in stone along Misbehaver's Way. Here are just a few:

- SilkWings are assigned professions suited to their limited set of skills as a tribe and begin work as soon as they have wings.
- SilkWing partnerships are designated by Queen Wasp and her sisters, and are binding unless the queen chooses to sever them.
- To preserve the dignity and unity of our two tribes, personal relationships between HiveWings and SilkWings are not tolerated.

- No trees are allowed in the Hives, neither planted in our terrariums or gardens nor portrayed in our art, in solemn commemoration of all the lives lost during the Tree Wars.

- To ensure their safe transit throughout the Hives, all SilkWings must wear bracelets designating their school or place of work at all times. Travel between Hives must be cleared with supervisors and local HiveWing authorities.

- All dragons must refrain from stealing or destroying property, especially that belonging to the queen or the other Hive rulers.

- All SilkWing and HiveWing hatchings must be registered with the appropriate Hive. HiveWing eggs must hatch within the Nest.

- Each SilkWing Metamorphosis must take place within the Cocoon.

SILKWING SCHOOL CURRICULUM

Most SilkWing classes are taught by HiveWings. We're told constantly how HiveWings usually learn everything we do but at a *much* younger age, just so we know to feel inferior from the egg. Key topics include:

- The History of the Tree Wars: or, How awesome Queen Wasp was to save the SilkWings from the horrible LeafWings and how SilkWings should be grateful to her and her tribe forever and ever

- Literature and Writing: or, How to read and write so your HiveWing bosses can tell you what to do and send you on errands and so you can read books from the library about how great Queen Wasp is

- **Math:** or, How to add up the few scales SilkWings are allowed to acquire and subtract all of them just to get the basic necessities for survival because, really, SilkWings should be happy to have jobs at all
- **Animal Studies:** or, Why don't we learn about all the animals that could kill you outside the Hives so you'll believe it is only safe inside
- **Physical Exercise:** or, HiveWings can fly long distances by age two and you silly SilkWings don't even grow wings till you turn six so go run around that racetrack for a while
- **Silk Studies:** or, Yes, fine, this is the one thing SilkWings can do that HiveWings can't so we'll let some SilkWings show you the basics of spinning, weaving, and web structures, but don't get any ideas

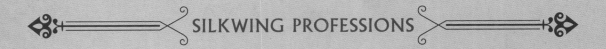

SILKWING PROFESSIONS

All SilkWing jobs are assigned — no choices or preferences allowed. HiveWings say it's because we're "overly sensitive" and "prone to fits of fancy." Apparently back before the Tree Wars it wasn't unusual for a SilkWing fresh from the Cocoon to take some time off from school and explore the continent with their new wings before deciding on a job.

After the wars, Queen Wasp put a stop to all that and told us we had to do the jobs we're assigned, or else. Dragons who are especially good at something, or just quick at their work, are often assigned tasks that are harder for them — and "troublemakers" usually are given the hardest jobs. Some of us think that's so we're all too busy and tired to wish for a better life.

- **Construction workers** break down old treestuff and reshape it to build or repair other parts of the Hive. This work is really difficult and can even be dangerous, but it's necessary. Ever since the Leaf Wars, there have been no trees to use to build new structures in the Hives.

- **Web workers** spin and repair the webs between Hives. These webs are home to all SilkWings and serve as bridges between Hives, enabling even wingless SilkWings to travel to other Hives (if they're allowed to . . .).

- **Spinners** create beautiful, artistic tapestries. The best spinners' work is in high demand by wealthy HiveWings, including Queen Wasp.

- **Weavers and dyers** create all kinds of threads and cloths for uses ranging from practical to decorative. Their work can be seen adorning the denizens of Jewel Hive, covering windows, or wiping up dragonet messes.

- **Servants** work in the homes, schools, and businesses of HiveWings performing any duties that their HiveWing employers request, including food preparation, dragonet care, and cleaning.

- **Performers** travel from Hive to Hive, putting on plays and concerts for HiveWings (and in some less restrictive Hives, SilkWings). The best performers are highly sought after and have a lot of opportunities to see more of the continent, so for some dragons this is a dream job, while others dread the idea of traveling far from family and friends.

Cricket,

I have been sorting through the books and scraps of paper hidden away in Wasp's quarters, and I found this, which I thought you might like for that book you mentioned.

I think it might be the last thing Queen Monarch ever wrote, and it gives our tribe some clues about what really happened to her, at long last. After she abdicated the throne, she vanished from sight. We never knew if she went on to a humble life among the rest of the population, or if she died in battle beside Queen Wasp. As we could perhaps have guessed, it was a little more sinister than that.

I always wished she'd cared more about us, but now I think she actually did. I wouldn't have made the choices she did — but I would have hated to be the one who had to make them.

— Tau

MONARCH
OF THE SILKWINGS

Am I the worst queen my tribe has ever had?

Or am I their savior?

Did I make a choice that saved countless SilkWing lives, or a terrible mistake that has doomed them forever?

Was I wise, faithful, and true? Or foolish and cowardly?

I really don't know. Can all of these be true at once?

I know I love my tribe. I love every dragonet and every heart and every scale on every wing. I thought I was following their destiny. I thought I was protecting them — I *was* protecting them.

But I did not expect to end up here, trapped in a room in Wasp Hive, guarded day and night, never to see my dragons again. I have this awful fear that an unfortunate "accident" awaits me any day now. And then my tribe will have no queen, and I leave no heirs. I've lived barely twenty years — I thought I had so much time for all of that.

Is this what Clearsight wanted? Truly?

I remember hearing stories about the Book of Clearsight all my life, mostly from my mother, Queen Diadem. She loved the tales about how Clearsight saved the tribes, over and over, during her life and long afterward as well. Sometimes the prophetic instructions were vague — a sense that there was danger along the coast, so everyone should shelter inland during the night of three full moons in the reign of Queen Cicada of the HiveWings. Or sometimes they were specific: apparently there was a full list of who should inherit the HiveWing throne stretching for generations yet to come.

Mother was impressed with that list; it saved a lot of infighting and bickering between HiveWing royal siblings. SilkWings, of course, rarely bicker — but each time a queen chooses her successor, there are inevitably hurt feelings. I was lucky I only had brothers so I never had to worry that Mother would choose someone else over me.

It's right there in the name she gave me, too, which makes me hope she knew I'd be a good queen from the moment I hatched. Monarch, the name of two of our greatest queens in SilkWing history. A name full of destiny and responsibility.

But maybe she was wrong. Maybe I'm not a good queen. Maybe I've ruined the name forever.

I wish I could leave these rooms and visit my tribe. Wasp says she is taking care of them. She says she is settling them in her new Hives, giving them jobs and food and schools and making sure they are all happy and healthy and safe. She says "they are being very good," which I do not actually find all that reassuring. Why are they "being good"? Are they scared? Or are they happy? I'd rather hear that they are happy.

I have a small window, so I can see my SilkWings flying around sometimes. I can see the beautiful webs they are weaving between the Hives and how they all work together to stretch them such impossible distances. I wish I could be up there with them.

I wonder if they miss me.

The only dragon I'm ever allowed to talk to is Wasp. She visits to give me updates on the Tree Wars. How many LeafWings she wiped out this week; how many forests she burned. (With *my* flamesilks!) How soon she expects to crush them under her talons.

Poor Sequoia. I really liked her. When I first met her and Wasp, I thought the three of us would be clever young queens together. We had those queen gatherings every few moons to smooth out any disputes before they escaped our claws. I was always so excited to see them. I'd bring a new kind of tea or lemon sugar crunches or peanut butter cookies. Everything is better with tea and sugar.

I suppose I should have worried more about how Wasp and Sequoia argued, and how it got worse with every meeting. Sequoia started to accuse Wasp of destroying trees, and Wasp would get so furiously defensive. I was always stuck in the middle.

And then Wasp came to a gathering with the news about the prophecy.

She told us the Book of Clearsight said "the time has come to unite the tribes. You must bring them all together under the leadership of one queen, Wasp of the HiveWings. Otherwise, a terrible fate will befall every dragon on the continent." That seemed clear enough, right? I thought Sequoia would agree, too!

After all, we don't have to understand Clearsight's instructions to know that they will keep us safe. We don't have to read them with our own eyes to have faith in them.

But Sequoia's faith was not like mine. She said that was "awfully convenient" and "suspicious that it never came up before." She wanted to see the words in the Book for herself, even though it has been For HiveWing Eyes Only for as long as it has existed!

Oh, there was a terrible fight. Wasp and Sequoia hissed and yelled and it made me so awfully anxious and sad. I hoped if I agreed to hand over my power to Wasp, it would calm them both down long enough for Sequoia to see sense. But it didn't; she got only angrier.

Still, I didn't think we'd end up at war. I didn't think Wasp would be so *violent* about all this.

My one consolation is that she does not believe SilkWings are any use on the battlefield. My tribe is not a part of the bloodshed and death. They are safe, thanks to me. If I had refused Wasp, for certain they'd have been slaughtered just like the LeafWings.

But then . . . Clearsight, *why* did you choose her to lead us?

If the tribes needed to have one queen, why not Sequoia instead? Maybe because Wasp was the oldest of us? But couldn't you see in your visions that Wasp might be a little scary? That she would take the tribes to war rather than let the LeafWings go?

Couldn't you see that I would end up like this, a prisoner cut off from my tribe?

It is heresy to write this, I know. I must have more faith, not less, to get through these trials. Maybe soon the Tree Wars will be over. Maybe then Wasp will let me out. I could live a normal SilkWing life; I don't need to be treated like royalty. I don't need power like she does. I would be happy to slip away, to disappear, if she would let me.

But it doesn't matter what happens to me. What matters is that my tribe is safe.

Clearsight, please protect them. Whatever you saw, whatever you meant with the words in your Book, please watch over them now.

I *do* believe in you, I do. I am sure you will guide them to the brightest future.

Even if I won't be there to see it, at least I know they will be all right.

∽◦€ LUNA'S HONEY DROPS RECIPE ≈◦∾

The Hives are famous for the wide variety of sweets their confectioners have developed over the years. Luna's favorites are called honey drops, and while she buys them at sweet shops, she did share this recipe from a failed attempt to make them herself in the hopes that a better cook could re-create them. She said hers were too sticky — maybe she used too much honey, or maybe the flamesilk globe she tried to heat it over wasn't hot enough. Be sure to ask a dragon at least as old as Luna to help you make these.

HONEY DROPS

- 5 parts sugar
- 4 parts water
- 2 parts lemon juice
- 3 parts honey
- A pinch of crushed ginger root (optional)

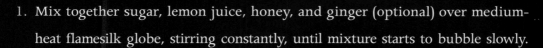

1. Mix together sugar, lemon juice, honey, and ginger (optional) over medium-heat flamesilk globe, stirring constantly, until mixture starts to bubble slowly.

2. Lift mixture away from globe so it cools a little and stir in honey (careful; honey burns easily!).

3. Heat mixture until a spoonful dropped into cold water creates threads that crack when you try to bend them.

4. Pour mixture into teardrop-shaped molds (or tiny shells, if you don't have molds) and let it harden.

5. Enjoy! (And save some for Luna if you get it right!)

CHAPTER 9

HIVEWINGS

QUEEN WASP
IN THE TEMPLE OF CLEARSIGHT

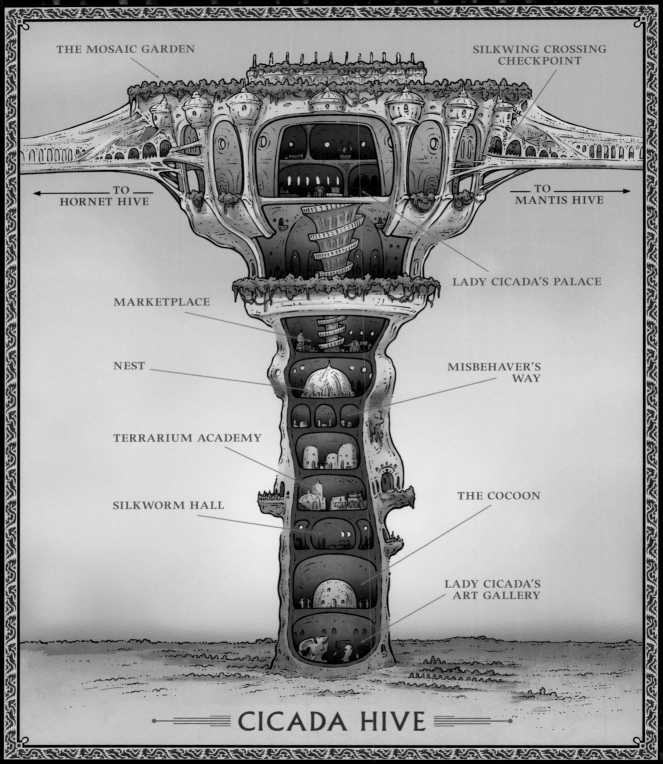

THE MOSAIC GARDEN

SILKWING CROSSING
CHECKPOINT

TO
HORNET HIVE

TO
MANTIS HIVE

LADY CICADA'S PALACE

MARKETPLACE

NEST

MISBEHAVER'S
WAY

TERRARIUM ACADEMY

SILKWORM HALL

THE COCOON

LADY CICADA'S
ART GALLERY

CICADA HIVE

HIVEWINGS

SCALES: red, yellow, and/or orange, always at least a few black scales

EYES: black, brown, red, orange, amber, yellow, or green

UNUSUAL CHARACTERISTICS: four wings that resemble dragonfly wings

ABILITIES: vary from dragon to dragon; examples include deadly stingers that can extend from their wrists to stab their enemies; venom in their teeth or claws; or a paralyzing toxin that can immobilize their prey; others can spray a boiling acid from a stinger on their tails

HABITAT: historically forest dwellers with a preference for caves and cliffs; since the Tree Wars they have been living in the nine Hives dotted around the continent of Pantala

DIET: the wild animals of the savanna, vegetables grown in the greenhouses, and confections made of sugar and honey

QUEEN: Queen Wasp

HIVEWING SCHOOL CURRICULUM

**WRITTEN BY CRICKET THE HIVEWING,
WITH SOME INSIGHT FROM NEW SILKWING FRIENDS**

While SilkWing schools offer general education prior to Metamorphosis and SilkWings complete on-the-job-training after their schooling ends, HiveWing schools require that students specialize at a young age. That specialization continues on into university studies. Many young HiveWings' paths are guided by their parents.

━━━ TERRARIUM ACADEMY COURSE LIST ━━━

Terrarium studies: An overarching term for coursework on soil, seeds, and water, terrarium studies takes up most of our time and is the lens through which all other classes are focused. By the time students are ready for university, we know what part of the agricultural process we will study there and what our job options are likely to be after we graduate.

Math: We learn the basics of addition, subtraction, multiplication, and division. We also learn how to calculate crop yields, how much water is needed to irrigate plots of certain sizes, and how to set prices based on supply and demand.

Science: We learn chemistry, biology, and botany, from soil composition to the benefits slugs provide for certain crops to the positive properties and uses of various plants.

Art: We learn to draw, paint, and make pottery to help us depict the plants we grow throughout their life cycles (no trees allowed!) and to create the pots we will use to grow our plants.

History: Taught once in a full moon, our history class mostly covers the triumphs of the HiveWings during the Tree Wars with an occasional (apparently entirely false) discussion of Clearsight's prophecies and how they help Queen Wasp guide our tribes.

Flight: As tiny dragonets, HiveWings are brought outside the Hives for flight class to learn how to use their wings and maneuver out in the open air and in all kinds of weather.

WASP HIVE

Home to Queen Wasp, the ruler of the HiveWings and SilkWings. The site of the Temple of Clearsight, it is the largest and oldest of the Hives, with many decorative touches including countless carvings of Queen Wasp. It is also harbors the secret prison of the flamesilks in a cavern underneath the Hive. Here a group of captive SilkWings with the ability to spin flamesilk were hidden away by the queen and forced to produce flamesilk threads to be sold to all the Hives.

Wasp Hive University admits only the very brightest and strongest students. The Librarian in the Temple of Clearsight is always selected from their ranks. Many eventually serve Wasp in her elite guard.

JEWEL HIVE

Ruled by Lady Jewel, this hive is well known for her love of the arts. One of its most famous features is the Glitterbazaar, a sprawling market of shops with a Salvation Statue at its heart. Jewel Hive University is the most artsy of the universities, with classes in all of the arts as well as in history and literature. Dragons who study there usually go on to teach at HiveWing and SilkWing schools or pursue careers as artisans.

BLOODWORM HIVE (DESTROYED)

Lady Bloodworm is known to be one of the cruelest of Queen Wasp's sisters. Most HiveWings with special abilities were sent to Bloodworm Hive University for training and experiments before going on to serve in the queen's guard. It's rumored that before the Hive was destroyed, they tested those powers on SilkWings who live in the Hive.

MANTIS HIVE

Ruled by the most famously bookish of Queen Wasp's sisters, Lady Mantis's hive has the second largest library in Pantala. Because of its university, which brings together the best and most loyal students from all the other universities to study together and come up with new, exciting ideas, Mantis Hive is known as the academic center of innovation. Its students go on to teach at other universities and to come up with the most useful inventions the Hives have seen since they were built.

Not too long ago, part of Mantis Hive collapsed. Some rumors blamed LeafWings, but it has been suggested that one of the many industrial experiments conducted here could have gotten out of claw.

CICADA HIVE

Known for its beautiful Mosaic Garden, filled with plants and home to the Salvation Wall, Cicada is a beautiful hive in which to enjoy nature. The Garden, which is very orderly and well maintained, is a reflection of Cicada Hive University, which trains farmers and gardeners for all the Hives.

HORNET HIVE

This hive is the center for commerce for HiveWings and SilkWings. It is where the offices of multi-Hive shops are based, with dragons here accounting for scales spent and goods flown throughout the Hives. Hornet Hive University trains dragons interested in commerce to run these shops, as well as to manage employees scattered across the continent.

VINEGAROON HIVE

Sitting on the edge of Beetle Lake and close to a bay, Vinegaroon is known for its wide variety of fish, which are served in a number of special dishes across the Hives.

Vinegaroon Hive University trains its students in zoology, teaching them about the animals of the savanna and the ocean to ensure that no species is hunted to extinction and that new species are accounted for and studied. They go on to lead research expeditions as well as hunting trips.

TSETSE HIVE

Tsetse Hive is where Queen Wasp decided to imprison any elderly dragons she found who couldn't be mind-controlled. Tsetse Hive University trains doctors and healers of all kinds, from basic skills needed to look after dragonets injured on the playground to doctors who treat the very ill.

YELLOWJACKET HIVE

This is the second-oldest Hive, after Wasp Hive. It is nearly as ornate as Wasp Hive and is constantly updating and upgrading its design. It is also home to several large manufacturing operations.

Yellowjacket Hive University is known to train HiveWings in engineering and manufacturing, from the architects who direct the work of SilkWing construction crews to the designers of glasses and lamps to the book printers.

Cricket, thanks for lending me your notes on HiveWing abilities! As far as I know, Bumblebee doesn't seem to have any stingers or venomous teeth or smelly powers, but she does seem very good at listening and communicating for such a tiny dragonet. That is, while she doesn't have a firm grasp on language yet, she can still get her point across through the use of volume and vigor, and occasionally tantrums (only sometimes!). Is being VERY LOUD a HiveWing power, by any chance?

— Willow

POTENTIAL HIVEWING ABILITIES

HiveWings have a number of special abilities. These powers are genetic and can be (but are not always) passed from parent to dragonet. While the physical features associated with these abilities are present at hatching, not all features are immediately evident. For instance, a dragonet with a tail stinger may have one of a few different abilities, and it can take time and careful coaxing for parents to figure out which it is. Similarly, a dragon's venomous teeth and claws, which are not dangerous to her relatives until she is about two years old, often aren't discovered until she starts school.

Queen Wasp, for instance, is known to have deadly stingers in her claws. What is not well known is that she also has a long, needle-sharp stinger in her tail.

Stingers: Many HiveWings have sharp stingers that extend from their wrists or claws and can be used to stab their enemies.

Venom: Some HiveWings have deadly venom secreted in their teeth, claws, or stingers. This venom is so powerful it can be used to kill large prey, such as antelopes or water buffalo. It is also extremely dangerous for dragons, including other HiveWings. Once this venom has breached the skin of a HiveWing's victim, it spreads quickly from the wound throughout the body and is usually fatal.

Nerve toxin: Certain HiveWings have stingers with a paralyzing toxin inside that can cause their victims to be totally immobilized. This is what is used to punish dragons forced to stand on display on Misbehaver's Way.

Acid: Some HiveWings have the ability to spray boiling acid at their enemies from their tail stingers, burning skin and other plant and animal materials. If sprayed into a dragon's eyes or into a wound, this acid can kill a dragon.

Stench: A rare few HiveWings have the power to emit a terrible smell of decay and sulfur.

LEGEND OF THE HIVE

Thousands of years ago, the first dragons arrived on the shores of the continent of Pantala. They were bedraggled and forlorn, weary and terrified. They came from many different tribes, including BeetleWings, LeafWings, RainWings, and SeaWings, and they had banded together to seek safety as far from the Distant Kingdoms as they could get. They fled from a terrible danger . . . but little did they know they were flying into something possibly even worse.

Their first night in this strange land, they collapsed to sleep on the beach, relieved beyond measure that they had reached a safe harbor at last. But as they all slept, the earth below them began to seethe with motion. Tiny legs crawled across their scales — and then more — and then more of them. The dragons awoke suddenly from their dreams into a true nightmare. They were covered in fire ants.

Their shrieks rose up to the three moons and they ran to the ocean, but even as they ran, more colonies of ants boiled up out of the ground and attacked. They marched up the dragons' legs and burrowed between their scales and dug their mandibles into

their skin. The ants didn't let go as the dragons plunged into the sea; they didn't try to save themselves. They held on like grim death, until at last the ants drowned.

But that was only the beginning.

The next morning, as the dragons were limping back to their campsite, they heard buzzing in the air, getting closer and closer. When they looked up, the sky was dark with bees. So many bees that they blotted out the sun. The bees descended and attacked, all at once, just as the ants had done. And again, the dragons were forced to flee into the bay and hide below the water.

Many of them would have drowned that day, were it not for their flamesilks, who burned the bees out of the sky.

The swarms of insects kept coming. The next wave was an army of venomous centipedes, followed soon after by a swarm of bombardier beetles, and after that by battalions of tsetse flies.

The insects killed dragon after dragon with single-minded, unwavering ferocity. Some of the dragons vanished in the night, never to be seen again. Others went down right in front of their friends, suddenly covered in assassin bugs.

Of course, the dragons fought back. They'd come too far to run away, and they could never return to the Distant Kingdoms.

So they fought to stay, but it seemed that whenever they struck down one group of attackers, another would instantly appear in its place. The insects were followed by hordes of snakes, a vast pride of lions, murders of crows.

These were not ordinary attacks. The animals moved like a single organism. If a scorpion was struck on one end of the battlefield, the scorpions at the far end somehow knew instantly. The crocodiles attacked simultaneously, targeting their victims with coordinated precision.

Was there someone mind-controlling all the creatures at once? So the dragon leaders believed, but if it was a dragon, they never showed themselves. Even after the newcomers spread across the whole continent, they found no evidence that any dragons had been there before them.

All they found was a plant with a sharp, unpleasant, omnipresent scent — a vine that seemed to wind around every tree, through every meadow, in every marsh. Pay attention: this is the breath of evil.

The stem of the breath of evil is dark red with veins of bright green.

The leaves of the breath of evil are bright green with veins of red like streams of blood. Each leaf is the size of a dragon talon; the edges are jagged and hard to the touch.

The flowers of the breath of evil are tiny and white and grow in clusters, nestled between the leaves.

The seed of the breath of evil hides in the heart of each flower, and it glistens a dark, dark red.

And this plant covered the entire continent of Pantala.

At first, the dragons were just clearing territory and making open space to sleep where they could set guards. They pulled up the vines to get rid of the smell. And that is how they discovered: as they destroyed the breath of evil, the attacks grew fewer and further between.

In areas where the vines were completely cleared, soon the attacks stopped altogether. The animals began to behave like normal animals, so long as they lived within the perimeter where there was no breath of evil.

And so the dragons set out to uproot the plant from every corner of the continent, and that is how finally, after much suffering, the Hive was defeated, and Pantala became safe for dragons forever.

Starflight,

Given all the lies we've been told about the Book of Clearsight throughout the years, I thought maybe it would be interesting to include a few true excerpts from the real, actual book. These are from a time when Clearsight's descendants used the book's prophecies to protect all three tribes. I don't know the full story of what happened when these particular prophecies came true, but since the tribes still exist, I'm guessing the Book saved us. (As books often do!) — Cricket

EXCERPTS FROM THE BOOK OF CLEARSIGHT

During the reigns of Queen Tawny and Queen Magnolia, there will come a dry season so hot and so long, it will feel as if the rains have deserted us forever. Beetle Lake will shrink to half its size; Lake Scorpion will become almost shallow enough to walk across. The leaves on the trees will curl and rattle with despair. Many dragons will move into the caves to escape the punishing heat.

But this you can survive. The rains will come again, and there are underground reservoirs you will discover to keep you alive.

The true danger will strike during the first, brief storm of the rainy season. Lightning will catch the dry trees like tinder, and the rain will stop before it can put the fires out. The fires will spread and rage through our forests like the fire-breathing dragons I used to know, unfurling flame from shore to shore.

If you do not take care, entire forests will be lost, and many dragons will die.

You cannot stop the lightning, but you can save hundreds, maybe thousands of trees and, I hope, all the dragons. During that dry season, you must build firebreaks all across the continent — gaps in the forests that the fires cannot cross. Plan them carefully and you can limit the damage. Ask my great-great-granddaughter Tortoiseshell to help you. She will be as clever as her namesake and have an eye for aerial mapping.

Then, when the first storm comes, take everyone underground. You will want to stay outside to dance in that rain, but you must resist (until the second storm, which will be safer). Stay in the caves until three days after the storm. That should protect all the dragons, if the firebreaks work as they should.

It is such a relief to write this — even as the ink sinks into the paper, I feel the weight of this future lifting. I see you reading this, going into the caves, and waiting patiently. I see you and the trees surviving, when this timeline was nothing but dark before.

Thank you, my darlings, for listening.

❀ — ✾ — ❀

In a time of many comets, when the night skies seem full of falling stars and Queen Zelkova rules from the southern forest palace, a pair of twins will hatch in the Royal Hatchery of the LeafWings. This is very important: **do not separate them!** There are timelines where one is sent to study at Dragon Ridge Academy and another remains with the queen; there are also timelines where one joins her father on a years-long expedition into the Poison Jungle. *Do not let this happen*. Wherever they go, whatever they choose to do, *they must stay together,* or the LeafWing tribe will be torn apart, and a disastrous civil war shall descend upon the continent.

❋ — ❋ — ❋

A note for Queen Silverwash: at the start of your reign, send out patrols to spin safety webs across all the large cenotes and sinkholes within two days' travel of your palace. This is generally a good idea for all SilkWing queens, but for some reason, your reign in particular experiences many wingless dragonets falling into these holes. The safety webs will save everyone a lot of heartache and rescue missions. (Perhaps remind your princes not to use them as trampolines, though!)

❋ — ❋ — ❋

I would advise no expeditions into the Poison Jungle for at least another five hundred years. I'm not entirely sure why, because those futures get cloudy very quickly, but it seems best to avoid it for as long as possible.

❋ — ❋ — ❋

It seems so strange to me that one day my descendants will number so many that they form their own tribe, but I am happy to see that it happens peacefully, and the dragons of Pantala continue to coexist in harmony. First queen of the HiveWings (can't say I love that name for our tribe, but all right, if you must): do not fly into Dragonfly Bay to poke the kraken! It will only be there for one rainy season, and it won't bother you if you don't bother it. It *looks* terrifying, but it is really just a little disoriented, hungry, and mostly harmless (although it will absolutely eat those three dragons you are thinking of sending to stab it with their toxin stingers. Not going to work! It is too big for any HiveWing powers to have an effect on it, trust me) (and wouldn't *you* eat a trio of annoying gnats that showed up and started jabbing at you?). Go fish on the other side of the continent instead and leave it alone!

CHAPTER 10

LEAFWINGS

QUEEN SEQUOIA
WITH PRINCESS HAZEL

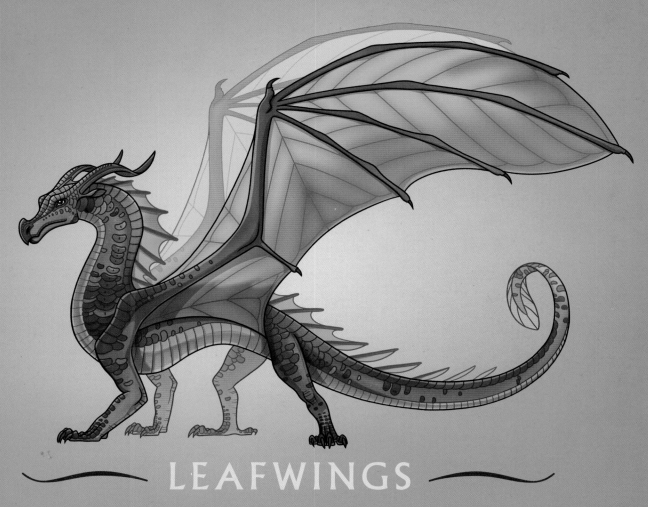

LEAFWINGS

SCALES: green and/or brown, sometimes with hints of gold, pink, or red

EYES: green or brown

UNUSUAL CHARACTERISTICS: two wings shaped like leaves

ABILITIES: can absorb energy from sunlight and are accomplished gardeners;
some have unusual control over plants, a power known as leafspeak

HABITAT: this tribe thrives anywhere there are trees,
but since the Tree Wars they have inhabited the Poison Jungle

DIET: panthers, frogs, insects, wild pigs, capybaras,
and anything else they can catch or gather in the jungle

QUEEN: Queen Sequoia

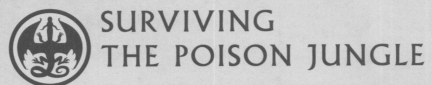

SURVIVING THE POISON JUNGLE

AS TOLD TO CRICKET BY HAZEL OF THE LEAFWINGS

THIS IS NOT AN EXHAUSTIVE GUIDE TO THE POISON JUNGLE. I just want to say that now, OK, Cricket?

LeafWings (PoisonWings and SapWings alike) are taught from a young age how to not die in the jungle. Newcomers would be wise to follow the leads of leafspeakers, who can persuade certain plants to leave dragons alone, but traveling with a leafspeaker is no guarantee of safety.

And also, while we *think* the things that are safe for LeafWings to eat or touch would be safe for all dragons, we can't really know for sure, can we?

Listen carefully and scan your surroundings!
In the Poison Jungle, *everything* is a threat. A smart dragon assumes any unidentified plant or animal could kill them and acts accordingly. Capybaras, for instance, aren't dangerous to dragons, but they can carry ticks that are — and if you spot one barking in distress, watch out for anacondas and other predators!

Avoid predators and dangerous plants!
There are plants that think dragons are delicious. Unless you want to spend half a day being digested by a Venus dragon-trap, you'd do well to avoid flowers that look like giant pink open mouths and smell delicious. If you *do* accidentally get eaten, hold still, pretend you're already dead, and maybe the plant will let you go — but if not, I sure hope you have a friend nearby who can try to get you out again!

Watch out for strangler vines, which would be more than happy to ensnare you — making you easy prey for all the giant cats and snakes that became even bigger and faster to survive the Poison Jungle.

Travel lightly but wisely!

Don't linger where you land, and don't hold on too tight. Pick your trees carefully — some are safe, some aren't, and even if a branch seems sturdy and not poisonous, the leaves or the moss growing nearby might not be. Definitely *never* land on (or touch or eat any part of) a sandbox tree. You've been warned!

Don't leave anything behind that a predator could use to track you, and don't make any loud noises that might draw a predator's attention. LeafWing dragonets practice stealthy jungle survival skills in the villages for a very long time before we let them stick a talon outside.

Pack smart!

Don't carry too much with you when you make your way around the jungle — you don't want to be weighed down when a panther is chasing you! It's wise, though, to fill your pouch with certain plants that can come in handy when you encounter the dangers of the jungle.

- Sleep lilies can be used on most creatures to knock them out, if you can get them to smell one, and a sniff or two is enough to calm down an anxious dragon.
- Mistletoe — both the pale white berries and the leaves — is highly poisonous to all mammals, including scavengers. One berry can knock out a jaguar — if you can get it to eat one!
- Chewing some ginger root before a difficult journey through the jungle can stave off the motion sickness from a particularly bumpy and twisty route.
- Need to get away in a hurry and not be followed? Crumble a few smoke leaves in your claw and toss them toward your enemy to create a cloud of smoke to confuse them.

Good luck!

This is not nearly enough information to get you through the Poison Jungle alive, but it might be enough to allow you to hang out near the outskirts till a LeafWing shows up to save you. Maybe? Hopefully!

An astonishing number of dragons, especially HiveWings, seem to think that LeafWings can't read. When I mention one of my favorite books, they give me a puzzled face, or say "You had BOOKS in the POISON JUNGLE?" or sometimes even "I thought you sinister LeafWings were too busy plotting revenge to learn to read."

(Which is treetop-level nonsense, by the way, since (a) my half of the tribe wasn't plotting anything except survival! and (b) if your entire tribe were constructing a plot together, of course it would be useful to know how to read so you can send one another scheming messages! And take notes on your sinister plot! By all the trees, I mean, seriously.)

But yes, we did have books in the Poison Jungle. One of the great things about living in a jungle, in fact — even a terrifying one full of plants that are trying to eat you — is that there are lots of resources for making books. Plant fibers, bark, sap for glue, wood pulp to make paper, even lots of ways to dye the covers. I love bookmaking and bookbinding; I'm going to do it forever, even when I'm queen one day!

And it's an important job, almost as important as being queen, because our tribe needs all the books we can make. The LeafWings lost so many libraries in the Tree Wars. We had to leave most of our books behind when we finally fled to safety.

But my great-grandmother Queen Sequoia managed to bring some of her personal library with her when she escaped, and so did many other LeafWings, luckily. In the fifty years since then, we have reconstructed as many books as the old dragons can remember. And we've written many more as well! Queen Sequoia believes that books are essential to a tribe's survival, and more important, to its soul.

So, to prove that LeafWings do read, and actually read enough to even have favorite books, I have conducted some interviews and compiled the following list of reviews for Starflight's guide.

— Hazel

FAVORITE BOOKS OF THE LEAFWINGS

THE LEGACY OF THE LEAFWINGS

It's a history of great LeafWing queens and achievements, and it was the first book I made sure to bring when we went into hiding. I find it helpful to read to remind myself that queens in the past had struggles, too, and yet the LeafWing tribe survived.

— Queen Sequoia

ASH OF GREEN GINGKOS

I've loved this one since I was a young dragonet, and I reread it every year around my hatching day. Ash is a brave, kind, funny heroine who is always dreaming up stories, and I especially love her relationship with Guava, the beautiful dragon who annoys her but is clearly her soul mate.

— Willow

THE COUNT OF MOUNT KUDZU

This book has *everything*: murder, revenge, more revenge, SO MUCH REVENGE. It's about a dragon who is unjustly imprisoned and spends his imprisonment planning his revenge and then escapes and *executes that revenge* and it's SPECTACULAR. (Sorry, Hazel, some of us were plotting revenge *and* learning to read . . . about plotting revenge!)

— Sundew

ROWAN AND JUNIPER

My favorite book used to be *The Count of Mount Kudzu*, but now it's this. I don't know why. It's just such a great story of two dragons falling in love who aren't supposed to. It would totally make me cry — if I ever cried, which I don't! — Bryony

THE EXCEPTIONALLY COMPREHENSIVE ENCYCLOPEDIA OF INSECTS FOR THE DISCERNING ENTOMOLOGIST

I love this book. Is that weird? Sorry if that's weird. It just has so many cool bugs in it! I could look at them and think about them all day! — Mandrake

MYSTERIOUS AND MYSTIFYING MURDERS

This is a compendium of baffling unsolved murders throughout the history of Pantala. It is fascinating to consider all the many different ways to murder a dragon and never get caught. I mean, from a purely theoretical standpoint, of course. — Cobra Lily

WHERE THE MOUNTAIN MEETS THE MOON

I absolutely love this book. It is full of magic and stories and a dragon on a quest to find out why he can't fly, and every time I read it, I feel like it's making me kinder and wiser and more thankful, which is the kind of queen I want to be. — Hazel

Starflight,

I found a hilarious thing to put in your guide. You would think that burning down an entire jungle would mean everything was destroyed, right? But no! When we went back and searched through the ashes, we found several LeafWing artifacts that survived the fire. Including a box that Queen Sequoia buried of "Archival LeafWing Documents: For Future Historians." Most of which is BOOORING, but! There are these letters between her and my mom and my grandmother! Which are amazing! Mostly because my mom sounds like a stompy, petulant, bad-tempered baby dragonet, ha ha ha. So I thought they were definitely worth preserving and publishing. Don't you agree?   *— Sundew*

Linden,

I had a terrible dream about you last night. I dreamed that you were clearing a space in the jungle for your new village and you found a root sticking out of the ground, but when you pulled on it, it was the horn of a HiveWing, which came surging out of the earth to attack you, followed by thousands more HiveWings.

I worry about you and the others all the time. I know you feel it was weak for us to go into hiding, but I couldn't bear to lose any more LeafWings, especially once I had only one granddragonet left. I hope you are being careful. I know you are; you were my best general, and I still trust you, even though you no longer follow me.

Please try not to draw Queen Wasp's attention here, to our last remaining hope of safety.

And please stay in touch. Even though you are starting your own village, I will always think of you as part of my tribe.

Safe branches,
Sequoia

Sequoia,

You can stop worrying about us. We are doing fine, and our plan to keep fighting Wasp is more of a long-term strategy. I've been thinking about my leafspeak, which I mostly use to grow food for my village or keep the scarier plants out. It's not very strong, but I've noticed that my daughter's is stronger than mine—perhaps because her father had some leafspeak talent as well. This makes me wonder how much stronger the gift could be, and what a brave dragon could do with such power.

Oh, right, I don't think I told you. I have a daughter now. Her name is Belladonna. I know it's not a traditional LeafWing name, but we are not going to be a traditional LeafWing village. We are going to devote our lives to ultimately winning the Tree Wars. All our dragonets will be named after powerful, ferocious plants, and we will train them to be fearless warriors. And one day, when they're ready, we'll strike back at last.

I hope when that day comes you will join us. Despite our differences, you are still my queen in my heart. And if I have to win this war without you, I will.

Strong roots,
Linden

Linden,

Thank you for your last update on the PoisonWing village. I'm so impressed with what you've managed to build and all your young dragonets. If you need anything from us that might help keep them safe, let me know. How is Belladonna's leafspeak progressing? She sounds like a branch off the old tree, as fierce and stubborn and brave as her mother. I hope you'll bring her to our next full-moon meeting. Are you still planning to marry her to that other leafspeaker? I think you said his name was Hemlock?

All is well in our village. Perhaps we could have a gathering for the New Year of the Trees and bring all the LeafWings together to celebrate? I know my dragons and your dragons often sneak into the jungle to see one another, but I am sure they would be happy to have a real reunion, just for a night, if you would be willing.

Safe branches,
Sequoia

SEQUOIA,

Your letters are NO LONGER WELCOME in the TRUE LeafWing village! I regret to inform you that my mother, General Linden, was killed by a gympie-gympie stinging tree while leading young dragonets on a safety training drill. We are all very sad and determined to live up to her legacy by DESTROYING the HiveWings and CRUSHING their stupid Hives!

I am the new leader of the true LeafWing village and I DON'T acknowledge your authority and I NEVER want to hear from you again, so go sit on a nettle and leave us alone!

— *Belladonna*

Belladonna,

I am so sorry to hear of your mother's passing. She was the bravest dragon I ever knew, and I truly loved her. I am sure you will be an equally strong leader, and I can see that you care deeply about the dragons under your wing. I urge you to stay in contact with me — a day may yet come when one of us needs the other's help. I am always here for you as a friend, even if you do not see me as a queen.

— *Sequoia*

SEQUOIA,

    GO SNORT A POISONOUS TOAD. I will never need your help!   — Belladonna

Belladonna,

    I have respected your wishes and not written to you in several moon cycles, but I hope you will accept this letter as a talon outstretched in friendship. We had some excess from our last harvest, so I am sending along a crate for your village, in case you might find any of this useful for your dragons. I believe it includes bananas, potatoes, yams, papayas, avocados, kumbu, and dragonberries as well as seeds for you to plant more, if you should want to.

    Please let me know if you ever change your mind and would be willing to meet — I still believe it would be ultimately beneficial for both our tribes.

From roots to canopy,
Sequoia

SEQUOIA,

    I KNEW you were spying on us, you ARROGANT PANTHER-BUTT-FACE! Keep your stupid snooty nose out of our business! So what if our entire harvest failed! It was stupid bad luck that all those weird insects got into it, that's all! We will just eat PIRANHAS and TIGERS like REAL WARRIORS until I can grow something else! Which will be any time now! We don't need your seeds or your pity food!

    But I am keeping it anyway because that'll show you! Ha! Don't you dare send anything else! We are doing GREAT!   — Belladonna

P.S. But if your sappy heart can't take it and you desperately have to send us another crate, could you include some mangoes next time?

Belladonna,

It has now been years since your mother's death, but I still think about her all the time. I know she would be proud of you and the village you've built and held together in her absence. I hope our occasional gifts are helpful, but I am sure you are right that you would be thriving even if we didn't exist.

I heard you are with egg, and it made me wish Linden could be alive to meet her grand-dragonet. I thought I would try once again to ask for a meeting. Linden and I used to meet every time a moon was full, at the island near the mouth of the Gullet River. Would you consider it, now that so much time has passed?

Safe branches,
Sequoia

Sequoia,

Fiiiiiiiiiiiiiiiiiiiiiiiiiiiiiiiiiiiiiiiine, you repetitive old bat. I'll be there. But don't think this means you get to boss me around or anything!

Also you should make your spies less obvious! One of them nearly got his snout stuck in our border fence the other day! We do not need to be watched constantly by SapWings!

I'll bring Hemlock to meet you if you bring some of those dried mangoes that were in the last crate.

Till the full moon,
Belladonna

VERY IMPORTANT ANNOUNCEMENT
TO BE PRINTED IN EVERY NEW SCROLL FOR THE FORESEEABLE FUTURE

TAKE NOTICE, ALL DRAGONS!!

STOP EATING SCAVENGERS!!!!!!!!!!!!!!

⭠RIGHT NOW!⭢
DO NOT EAT THEM!

SCAVENGERS CAN THINK!
AND TALK! AND YELL AT US!

Hello, dragons! My name is Wren and I am a scavenger, although we prefer to be called humans. I speak Dragon and understand you all, and some of my friends are learning your language, too. So just imagine picking up a delicious snack, and then suddenly the snack shouts: "Dragon, no! Bad dragon! Don't eat me! I don't want to be your snack!" Wouldn't that be very upsetting? Yes. Avoid this problem by leaving humans alone! We are quite clever and we also don't like it when you burn our villages or step on us.

Tell your friends! No more scavenger eating!

~~Unless they are mean old toads who used to live in Talisman~~ (OK, no really, absolutely nobody.)

Thank you very much!   — Wren of the Humans

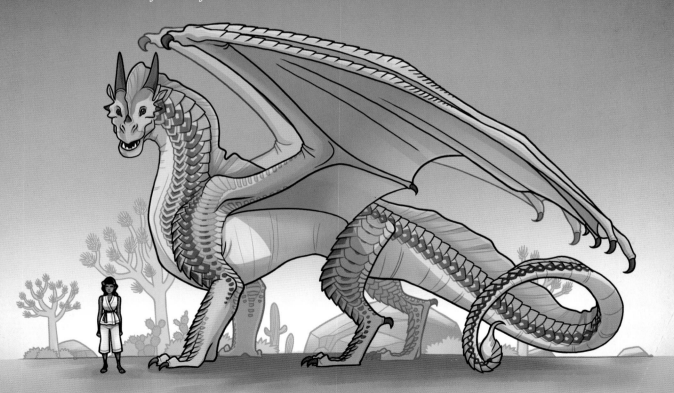

ROSE AND SMOLDER

DISCOVER THE WORLD OF
WINGS of FIRE

→ THE DRAGONET PROPHECY →

TUI T. SUTHERLAND
Wings OF FIRE
THE DRAGONET PROPHECY

TUI T. SUTHERLAND
Wings OF FIRE
THE LOST HEIR

TUI T. SUTHERLAND
Wings OF FIRE
THE HIDDEN KINGDOM

TUI T. SUTHERLAND
Wings OF FIRE
THE DARK SECRET

TUI T. SUTHERLAND
Wings OF FIRE
THE BRIGHTEST NIGHT

→ THE JADE MOUNTAIN PROPHECY →

Wings OF FIRE
MOON RISING

TUI T. SUTHERLAND
Wings OF FIRE
WINTER TURNING

Wings OF FIRE
ESCAPING PERIL

TUI T. SUTHERLAND
Wings OF FIRE
TALONS OF POWER

TUI T. SUTHERLAND
Wings OF FIRE
DARKNESS OF DRAGONS

→ THE LOST CONTINENT PROPHECY →

TUI T. SUTHERLAND
Wings OF FIRE
THE LOST CONTINENT

TUI T. SUTHERLAND
Wings OF FIRE
THE HIVE QUEEN

TUI T. SUTHERLAND
Wings OF FIRE
THE POISON JUNGLE

TUI T. SUTHERLAND
Wings OF FIRE
THE DANGEROUS GIFT

TUI T. SUTHERLAND
Wings OF FIRE
THE FLAMES OF HOPE

HOME BASE

SCHOLASTIC

Download on the
App Store

GET IT ON
Google Play

Book One
THE DRAGONET PROPHECY

Book Two
THE LOST HEIR

Book Three
THE HIDDEN KINGDOM

Book Four
THE DARK SECRET

Book Five
THE BRIGHTEST NIGHT

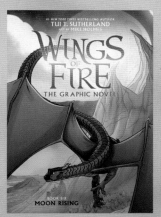

Book Six
MOON RISING

LEGENDS & WINGLETS

WINGS OF FIRE LEGENDS
DARKSTALKER

WINGS OF FIRE LEGENDS
DRAGONSLAYER

WINGS OF FIRE
THE WINGLETS QUARTET
THE FIRST FOUR STORIES

INTERACTIVE

WINGS OF FIRE
FORGE YOUR DRAGON WORLD

WINGS OF FIRE
THE OFFICIAL COLORING BOOK

TUI T. SUTHERLAND is the author of the #1 *New York Times* and *USA Today* bestselling Wings of Fire series, the Menagerie trilogy, and the Pet Trouble series, as well as a contributing author to the bestselling Spirit Animals and Seekers series (as part of the Erin Hunter team). In 2009, she was a two-day champion on *Jeopardy!* She lives in Massachusetts with her wonderful husband, two awesome sons, and two very patient dogs. To learn more about Tui's books, visit her online at www.tuibooks.com.

JOY ANG is an illustrator and animator known for her work as a character designer and title card painter for the Cartoon Network series *Adventure Time*. She has also created art for a number of children's books, working with publishers like Houghton Mifflin, Random House, and Bloomsbury. When she's not working, she's most likely spending time with her family and friends, gardening or foraging.

MIKE SCHLEY is a visual artist and cartographer who develops imaginative worlds for book and game publishers. When not making art, he enjoys hiking the forests and mountains of the Northeast United States, near where he lives in Philadelphia.

MAARTA LAIHO spends her days and nights as a comic colorist, where her work includes the comics series *Lumberjanes*, *Adventure Time*, and *The Mighty Zodiac*. When she's not doing that, she can be found hoarding houseplants and talking to her cat. She lives in the woods of Maine.